GUILTY
with an Explanation

GUILTY
with an Explanation

A Story of Becoming

Trevor Toop

RESOURCE *Publications* · Eugene, Oregon

GUILTY WITH AN EXPLANATION
A Story of Becoming

Resource Publications
An Imprint of Wipf and Stock Publishers
199 W. 8th Ave., Suite 3
Eugene, OR 97401

www.wipfandstock.com

PAPERBACK ISBN: 978-1-5326-5215-8
HARDCOVER ISBN: 978-1-5326-5216-5
EBOOK ISBN: 978-1-5326-5217-2

Manufactured in the U.S.A.   04/19/18

Peterborough, about 1970

Dedicated to the memory of Allan Trevor Toop. My father might rightfully have been a bitter man. He inherited circumstances in life by which he had an uphill battle from the start, worked way too hard, yet ended up leaving the world a better place than he found it. His only brother was proof that two people born into the same circumstances, can make very different choices. My Dad was of a kindly disposition and was one of those rare people who knew something about everything. If you see some good in this story, making its way into the world through the small and quiet virtues, then you know something of my father. I hope some of those good qualities may have rubbed off on me.

"How do you plead," asked the judge?
"Guilty or not guilty"?

The defendant looked down at
his hands and paused.

"Your Honor, I wish to plead guilty,
with an explanation," he said.

"The heart is deceitful above all things,
and desperately wicked: who can know it?"

—JEREMIAH 17:9 (KJV)

Contents

Acknowledgments

~

A book results from a lot of thinking. Though I don't know for sure I imagine it is somewhat akin to giving birth. It's a process, and there are many people who are witness to the long and somewhat arduous period of gestation. I would therefore like to thank the following people:

Amparo Cifuentes of Toastmasters, for helping to find my voice. It's a way of clarifying what you think.

Karen Stiller, for reading a draft and encouraging me to squeeze the story a little harder.

My wife, Abir, for putting up with the vicissitudes of living with an artist. They are a complicated bunch, I know. And they think too much.

My lovely daughters Elizabeth, Rima, and Petra for adding joy and purpose to my life.

My Editor Matthew Wimer for his readiness to help make the process of bringing a book about, easier.

Author's Introduction

~

Guilt is a concept which has fallen on hard times. What the self-esteem industry has managed to destroy over the course of a generation, is the notion that sometimes, people are just courting trouble – it's part of the human condition. During a dozen-year stretch of my career, I was a freelance court sketch artist, which required me to closely study the demeanor of those who have been accused of sometimes heinous crimes. One trial in Calgary Alberta for example, featured a sixteen-year-old boy who had inexplicably chopped up his parents with an axe in the middle of the night. The crime scene had so much blood on the walls that police initially assumed that there had been a shotgun involved. Do you know what a murderer looks like? I don't. This kid was hardly shaving, and he looked like butter wouldn't melt in his mouth. In fact, I would say that most murderers would be indistinguishable from anyone you might pass in the street. The common thread might be that while they lack a sense of guilt, their self-esteem seems to be in pretty good order. In light of this, you could say that the value of guilt in our present society might be underrated.

The Bible's third chapter of Genesis, the Fall of Man, sets out the human dilemma in graphic terms. Unlike the animals, who operate purely from instinct, we get to choose what we want, rationalized into the future. Human beings alone come equipped with a nagging sense of right and wrong, and the problems in the world today, spring from the times we betray that God-given instinct – it all echoes back to a vision of Adam first reaching for that apple. If we are to be honest, we all bear the flesh of the Old Adam. The best verdict we might come up with for ourselves, might be guilty with an explanation. We didn't mean to. Or sometimes, we did.

But life teaches. There is that thorny thing about consequences. As Margaret Thatcher once famously observed, "The facts of life are conservative." My mother had her own somewhat folksy version of this. She used to say, "Twenty years of living will knock some of those ideas out of your head. . ." In deference to my mother I would have to admit, if I have accrued any wisdom to this point, it may be from every dumb mistake I have ever had to pay for the hard way.

That is why it is a good thing to have mentors, leaders, active fathers, role models, even, dare I say, heroes. They light the way in the darkness. They show us that there is a role in faith that stretches beyond the touchy-feely, because in the end, we exist not just in our heads, but in the real world. Unfortunately, the real world is also a place which is increasingly closing doors on men and telling them they have no worthy function. To strip them of an honorable place, is also to deprive society of what men can be at their best. The case for fathers for example, might best be stated by anyone unfortunate enough to have struggled through life without one.

This book is a coming of age story, and as such it is unapologetically geared toward men. It's the subtext of rumination and experience over the course of a few decades. If you want to stand with the truth, you are going to get some blood on you, because the war on truth has been raging ever since the day when a serpent first showed up in a garden, and the harrowing of that equation always comes down to self. It seems to be, that while women arrive at womanhood via the course of nature, a boy comes to know he is a man when he is tested in some kind of epic struggle where he must stake his ground and choose the hill he is ready to die on. In this story I have revisited life afresh through the eyes of a twelve-year-old who must find his own way after his father's death, and judge what is worthy. Some conclusions he arrives at may be considered old-fashioned—I would prefer to think of them as time-worn truths, not lightly to be abandoned. They are things I know now as a man that I wish I could go back and give as wise counsel to my twelve-year-old self. Be watchful and prepared, for there be dragons. I think I would tell myself to read Ephesians chapter six and commit it to heart because it is going to be on the exam.

Because this is a story of good and evil, I have necessarily left the characters unvarnished, which should not be considered an endorsement of position. For the faint of heart, I apologize if some indelicacies offend, but to sanitize the characters would rob the story of its meaning. I have therefore endeavored to be as true to my own experience of life as I can manage, following the maxim which I believe is attributed to Eudora Welty, "I write fiction in order to tell the truth." Any resemblance to actual persons, living or dead, or actual events is purely coincidental.

Trevor Toop, Oakville, Ontario, 2018

Prologue

~

People like to argue about whether God exists, but when you get them on the topic of whether evil exists, they fall strangely silent. Take God out of the equation, and you can do the math yourself on who's left to blame. Accordingly, people mostly talk about justice in the abstract – it's safer that way. Whether I am guilty is a question that never occurred to me before the spring of 1972. I was just twelve. From that point onward, I have lived my life as one wishing to be absolved, and it has made me careful. Looking back, I can see all that I did, combined with all I could not do. Was I guilty? You can decide. Life can be hard to take back. This is my explanation.

I

~

Moses

I just couldn't keep my eyes off his fingernails. They were purposely grown out long and unapologetic. The edges were brown
and crusted with cavernous ridges, and the ends terminated in a
rough curve like a talon. He traced the calculations written in the
matchbook cover, slowly and deliberately like he had done this a
thousand times before. We knew what Moses was there for. He
had come for our mortal souls. Moses' eyes pierced through his
wiry brows like high beams coming at you through a windshield
at night. "You boys know what a googolplex is? It's the biggest
number ever figured. Biggern'n a million. Bigger'n a trillion. You
know how big that is? Well, I'll show you," he said, without pausing
for assent. "The moon is 238,857 miles from earth." He scanned
the cryptic pencil scratching, scribed in diminutive figures on the
inside of the matchbook, to see if he had quoted the right statistics,
and continued. "Now if you boys was to make a pile of dollar bills
a googolplex high. . . ." Moses launched into one of his spiritual
conversation starters, a series of prepared questions which were
contrived to browbeat the listener into a 'personal decision' to follow Jesus Christ in this life in order to secure residency in the next.

Me and my best friend Jimmy knew what was coming, but we had agreed to meet Ricky that Saturday morning by the World War II cenotaph, beneath the shadow of the bronze angel whose sword was raised triumphantly against the cringing figure of evil. The inscribed names of those who had saved the world before us stared across at us expectantly, beside a plaque that read, "*In memory of those who died defending mankind from evil. Their names ever shall endure.*" We were kids, and we knew about Moses, but we sat, squirming and trying to play along politely like you had to for adults. Moses was eldest brother of the Northey clan and he came in from the farm every Saturday to save souls. Why had we not remembered? I pinched my forearm above the freckle and left a blue mark.

On the other side of town, a diminutive rotund figure carefully levelled off a cup of puffed wheat from a large bulk bag under the watchful eye of his mother, who was tying a kerchief over her hair in preparation to leave. She appraised his measurement as if in question, and her sharp eyes followed as he mixed scoops from a large bag of skimmed milk powder with tap water. "Aw Mom, why can't we get regular milk like the *other* kids" Ricky whined. "This kind always gets lumpy and gross." "The starving kids in Africa are happy to drink that kind of milk," his mother noted curtly, pinching him on the back of the ear. We were twelve and Africa was always thrown up in our face to show how good we had it. Now Ricky's Mom was a cleaning lady, and his Dad pumped gas. It was the only job they would ever have, or would ever imagine, and life would just have to adjust. Her favorite aphorism was, "Wish in one hand and piss in the other and see which gets full first." Ricky was a dreamer but according to his mother's best advice, his dreams were rationalized within the possible. Sometimes he fantasized that when he grew up, he was going to move to Africa. In Africa people got all kinds of stuff for free and they didn't even have to do anything. But mostly he fantasized about finding bottles on the side of the road that he would trade in for penny candy.

"I have to go to the Moores and clean this morning," his mother continued, her cigarette ash dangling precariously from the corner of her mouth. "Check out that new car in the driveway," she harrumphed, "I seen the inside of their house and I know a few things. They think their you-know-what don't stink but their farts give them away. I bet they wonder about our car," she ventured, glancing proudly at the newly waxed Lincoln Continental in the driveway. Ricky's Dad had already left for his job pumping gas, but he had to walk. Ricky's mom had the lockdown on the family budget and the family larder. What she savored most in life, was revenge in the form of a few flashy possessions, wrung from a stringent family budget and fastidiously used, yet stridently poked in the eyes of the town just the same.

She didn't yet know that Ricky had lost his library book and owed one dollar and sixty-five cents according to the slip that the librarian issued for parents. Ricky was sweating because he had to take out a book for his school project, so he arranged to meet his friends there to borrow a library card and avoid a hiding, at least for now. His friends would likely give him a noogie, or even a wedgie, but it would be worth it, he thought. He hopped on his bike, with his empty army surplus knapsack strapped on his back and looked furtively at his watch. "Oh man," he said to himself, "I forgot to pee"! Without turning around, he peeled down the block, already breaking into beads of perspiration.

By this time Moses was already in full swing. "Boys," he said as he approached his destination with our souls in view. "Now if you was to spend a googolplex number of years in Hell, there ain't nothing to buy you out except fer blood. You know about *the* blood?" he asked, eyeing his prizes warily. We both looked at the cross brazened on the shield of the bronze angel but could not answer. "For the wages of sin is death; but the gift of God is eternal life, *praise-God-Romans-six-twenty-three*. . . You ever heard tell of the sinner's prayer"? We broke into a sweat wondering when Ricky would arrive. The angel's sword dangled above our heads, casting a shadow in the grass like a sundial. We instinctively scanned our watches.

2

~

Scriptum Est Enim

Ricky meanwhile had stopped to pick up a cache of pop bottles that a bunch of careless teenagers had cast aside the night before, near the cold ashes of a fire by the river road. "Man," he said to himself as he picked through the cigarette butts and fresh dew. "They gotta be nuts. These bottles are worth two cents each"!

He dislodged a gooey earthworm from one of the empties with a stick, looked disapprovingly at the carelessly smashed bottles on the ground, and then quickly stuffed the rest into his empty knapsack. His thoughts roamed to the Quick-Check corner store where he was going to trade in those six bottles on three-for-a-penny candy. That would be thirty-six of something. Jawbreakers or black babies? He wondered to himself. Or maybe some of those marshmallow strawberries, if he ate them first they wouldn't get stuck together in the brown bag. He got on his bike and peddled for the library. He still had to pee.

On the way he saw Roy, riding his new bike, and he pedaled faster to come up alongside. Now if you wanted to pile on to Roy, it was easy, and Roy wouldn't even notice. Roy was what the mothers winked and referred to, as 'simple', a perpetual innocent, who would never progress beyond the cognitive level of a six-year old. His bike was his most prized possession, a kids' version of a decked-out pimp-mobile, complete with high handlebars, a wire basket in back of the banana seat to carry stuff, and plastic discs with psychedelic patterns clipped onto the spokes that made the wheels seem as if they were turning backwards and forwards at the same time. "Hey Roy. . ." Ricky drawled in exaggerated tones, "*Nice bike*"! Roy flashed a bright white smile from behind his thick glasses, not knowing he was being egged on. "My Mom gave it to me" he beamed, taking the bait, "It's got *everything*." He rode away in obvious pleasure as Ricky cackled to himself, enjoying not being the butt of the joke this time. "Man, that kid is two bricks short of a full load," he mused in derision. Meanwhile, Ricky's ancient hand-me-down bike creaked along, belying the need for an oilcan and a spring tune-up. He had heard that Roy didn't even have to go to a real school; his school was like crafts and field trips, every single day. "I bet he doesn't even have to clean up his own room," he thought to himself. For a brief moment he was suffused with envy.

Ricky arrived at the cenotaph with the usual flair, full-speed, then a dramatic circular skid that he thought made him look like Evel Knievel. His abrupt arrival caught Moses in mid-sentence, temporarily lost for words. In that crucible of hesitation, we briefly considered our mortal souls, and then mounted our bikes at a run.

"You brood of vipers. Who told you to flee from the wrath to come?" Moses called out after us, spittle spraying down his ample white beard. Moses tucked the matchbook with the written figures carefully into the pocket of his bib overalls. As he ambled toward a young couple holding hands on a nearby bench, the shadow cast from the sword of the angel inched incrementally forward in the grass.

"Hey guys, you bring your library card?" Ricky asked. "Yeah" Jimmy replied, "but it's gonna cost you. Dibs on your empties" he smiled, having noted the clinking of glass in Ricky's knapsack. We were heading expectantly toward the end of sixth grade, the adventures of summer were coming into distant view and we had plans on our minds. "Guys, I gotta pee" Ricky whined. "Oh, man, I'm gonna piss myself." He tumbled down the stairs at a loose gallop, hands already fumbling with his fly, while we went upstairs to borrow his book.

Over the portal of the library a large stone tablet proclaimed, "*Scriptum Est Enim*," which I was told is Latin for "It is Written." Inside, and with the same sense of surety was Mrs. Sawyer, putting the world in order, dusting off the inherited knowledge of the universe, and clucking to herself as she re-shelved a book. "The Dewy Decimal System" she muttered. "Everything in its place. You'd think they would learn." Mrs. Sawyer pondered all the known data in the world, saved up under her control. If they lost all this knowledge, they would have to make the same mistakes all over again, she mused. The library is the clean version of the history of human error, all saved up in one place. You can't lose books because somebody might need those facts and then what? I am a guardian of the safety of the world, she thought to herself as she straightened her bun. She anticipated the invidious tasks of the upcoming day with a martyr's sense of duty, sighed at the thought of those who would try her patience, and deftly tucked a greying strand of hair behind her ear.

We approached the kiosk in hushed terms, the first customers of the day. We knew Mrs. Sawyer. This was her cathedral, the place in which her soul expanded with authority, exercising strict and worthy judgment over a congregation of tidy books and the inconvenient public. "Quiet boys" she cautioned, "this *is* a library. May I help you?" she offered crisply. We followed the Dewy Decimal system recipe card that she handed us and went to track down Ricky's book. Meanwhile downstairs Ricky burst through the bathroom door, fumbling with his fly. He collided with an unexpected figure on the way out, just as his eager bladder released a warm spray of pungent liquid, which darkened his jeans and trickled down to the floor. The other figure was Bart Wilson, a husky older teenager in a jean jacket who reeked heavily of cigarettes. We knew enough about Bart to purposely walk a long city block just to avoid him. Bart looked down in momentary recognition at the stream of warm pee that was trickling over his brand-new Adidas running shoes. His countenance flared in anger. Meanwhile Ricky was standing agape with his offending equipment still in hand. "Kid," hissed Bart as he stared down into Ricky's terrified eyes, "you're dead"!

3

~

The Weather Report

I should introduce myself. My name is Jacob. This story is about the year in my life where things changed. When you are a kid most things don't really matter very much—until they do. And when they do, they will matter a lot and your life will never be the same. It was a time which placed a judgement on me that I have weighed and sweated to be worthy of ever since.

I had a lot on my plate. My Dad had died the year before and it was just me and my Mom, who was trying desperately to adjust to life as a young widow. We were both suffering, but it was that weird kind of shared suffering where you are both together and alone without wanting to be either. We didn't talk about this stuff at home. I was quickly finding out that while suffering can be general and oblique, grief is private, pointed, and mysterious.

My grandma came to stay with us, to help out with laundry and cooking while my mom was at work. Grandma was mildly entertaining, and I could not quite figure out if she was totally nuts, or just playing her cards close to her chest. Grandma, whether from lack of knowledge or whim, seemed to vary between two different things—pancakes and chocolate chip cookies. Her passion was to sit watching all-star wrestling on TV, which she called her "rassling." Dressed in her leopard-patterned robe and curlers, she would sit in front of the TV with her stockings rolled down to her ankles, calling out the action and shaking her fist as the struggle between good and evil went another round. Grandma insisted that the wrestling was real. "Listen," she would say, as you tweaked the bunny ears on top of the TV console for her, "If someone threw *you* down on the floor like that, there would be nothing fake about it"! This observation I had to weigh against my Grandma's *other* sage claim. Sometimes while navigating the dial, she would linger momentarily on the weather report, then turn suddenly as if to impart a great secret. "Don't you know," she would confide, gazing at me darkly, "the *government* makes the weather. They got us all fooled"! Then she would click back to the wrestling, sit down and shake her fist at the screen once again. "Hey, that's not fair. Is the referee blind? Bastards"!

My Dad had been the high school maintenance man. He died from a sudden brain aneurism and was found by the security guard, lying on the floor beside his toolbox as if he had fallen asleep with work still left to be done. I could not believe my Dad was gone. I was marginally getting by, as one in a dream where you know you are sleeping but cannot wake up. My friends didn't know what to say really, except for how much my situation sucked. Mainly we just hung out and did stuff together. The town in which we lived was small and pretty average, which was ok only because we didn't have much else to compare it with.

We should have known Ricky would bring us some kind of disaster, but we were used to carving out our own space—the world of adults was one long list of arbitrary authorities around whom we had to navigate. As we fled the library, Mrs. Sawyer cackled after us. "Boys. *Boys.*" Bring back that book! Don't think I can't track you down"! But we had long made our getaway in a cloud of dust. Bart Wilson stood outside, shaking his fist. "Hey girls . . .," he called out after us, mocking. "Payback is going to be fun"!

4

~

In the Garden

After our clean escape, we had more practical considerations to take care of; Ricky and his wet pants. "Oh man, you're such an ass-wipe," Jimmy laughed. "I can't believe you actually pissed yourself"! We briefly considered our options and decided that the best thing to do would be to go over to my house where we could hose Ricky off in the yard and hang his clothes out to dry. We were planning a sleepover outside in my pup tent, anyway.

It was the beginning of the May twenty-fourth weekend, and the air was still breezy, even though the sun had come out. We got into the back yard and jeered at Ricky as he stripped down to his skivvies and demonstrated that when attention knocks at the door, dignity flies out the window. He took off his shirt, swinging it around in the air and swiveling his hips in his best imitation of an exaggerated strip routine. He unbuckled his jeans. "Feast your eyes boys," he mocked as he shimmied them off and tossed them on the grass. "Prime beef, ladies only"! Ricky was an ample target and we guffawed as Jimmy turned the hose on him. He jiggled like a bowl of cold Jell-O as the water streamed over his body, washing away the evidence of what had happened that morning.

Just at that moment Kevin Moore emerged through the back gate. Kevin was two years older than us, the edgy kid whom we partially feared, but hung out with anyway. He was a good six inches taller than any of us and was proudly nursing a small cluster of fluffy blonde hairs on his upper lip, which he steadfastly refused to shave. Kevin was convinced his somewhat pale version of a mustache made him look like Chuck Norris and he turned his head as he arrived, to show off his profile. "How's my 'stache looking today," he enquired while stroking it with his fingers profusely? "Hey Kevin, you think if you play with it, it will grow bigger?" chirped Ricky innocently? We all guffawed. "Shut up pin-dick"! snapped Kevin as he punched Ricky in the arm. "Nobody asked you anyway"! Ricky looked momentarily confused. "But you. . .?" he protested, before Kevin punched him in the arm yet again. It never occurred to us that Kevin hung out with us only because we were more willing dupes than friends his own age. We liked hanging out with him partially because he was older—and because Kevin had ideas. . . 'Too many ideas,' my mother had noted. "Listen up, juveniles," Kevin announced, "you want to help me with a job? It will be really cool, better than firecracker day even"! Firecrackers for Kevin allowed his creative imagination to roam to the more destructive ranges of adolescent behavior, and we could not imagine what job he had that could top the unfettered twenty-fourth of May Victoria Day long weekend that involved playing with fire and generally blowing things up.

Kevin suddenly turned his head to the side, stopped dead in his tracks, and held one hand up to his lips as if to silence us. His eyes bugged out and he frantically beckoned with the other hand. We approached the cedar hedge that bordered with the neighbors. . . and took in what Kevin was staring at. It was something none of us had ever set eyes on before.

5

~

Better than Sears Catalogue

Our new neighbors were self-proclaimed hippies. We had not seen much of them from the day their VW Beetle with psychedelic flower decals first appeared in the driveway, when they came over in their flip-flops and proudly presented my mother with a plant. They were both safely below thirty, and dressed in matching tie-dye shirts, he with exaggerated pork chop sideburns, and she with a neat and fashionable shag cut. They spent a good deal of time sequestered in their back yard behind the cedar hedge, and occasionally a strange-smelling smoke drifted through the foliage into our yard. "Whatever are they cooking on their barbecue?" my mother would venture. When we crept over to the portal Kevin had uncovered, we peeked through and saw an empty glass with a straw by the lawn chair, a folded Mother Earth News magazine sitting undisturbed, and bending over some geraniums, the neighbor lady, dressed in her flip flops. . . and nothing else. We had never seen a bare-naked lady before, and a brief scrimmage broke out around the portal, as we shoved and whispered, fighting for a view. "Oh man," hissed Ricky, "this is better than Sears Catalogue, even! C'mon guys, lemme look, no fair"! Kevin suddenly glanced down at Ricky's clinging wet undergarments and made an unfortunate observation. He ribbed me, pointed and guffawed, while

Ricky turned crimson and used both hands as a fig leaf. Jimmy and I looked at each other in silent recognition. We had no language by which to understand what was happening in our loins, except that it concurred with a conflicting mixture of thrill and shame. "Honey," called our neighbor's husband from inside, "can you grab me an apple"? Her lips turned up with a sagacious smile, and she picked up her magazine and empty glass, and headed for the house. "Did you get a good look, boys?" she quipped in a sotto voice, as her pink form swept past our portal. With a toss of her hips, she flipped us the bird without so much as a backward glance and sashayed out of view.

The "job" Kevin told us about, came with no details, just a promise that whatever it was would be worth it. We headed down by the quarry on the edge of town. "He said meet him here at three" Kevin informed us. We had no idea who 'he' was, so we huddled together on a stump and waited. Soon a beat-up red pickup truck pulled up spewing dust and braked to a stop. A somewhat tired looking man of about fifty got out, and without explanation, flopped down the tailgate and deposited at our feet, two industrial-sized cans of gasoline and a chain saw. He looked at us intently, weighing up the unexpected extra numbers, then seemed suddenly satisfied. He produced a flask from his inner jacket and took a pull on it. "Well, boys," he said. "I think you know what you gotta do. See these trees here? All this lot has got to be developed. I need these trees out of here by the end of the weekend," he said, gazing at us intently as if to gauge our response. "If I git back here on Monday morning and these trees is gone, it'll be forty dollars in your pockets," he informed us, before getting back into the pickup, and taking off in a cloud of dust.

We looked at each other dumbfounded not believing our good luck. That afternoon, we took turns hacking and destroying with wanton abandon as only teen boys can, getting an impromptu lesson both in how to operate a chain saw, and how to dodge a falling tree. Suddenly Kevin stopped and mopped his sweaty brow. "Man, this is too much work"! he said. "I think we should do a *shortcut*." He looked at us pointedly, then opened up one of the gas cans, and started to slosh gasoline behind him as he traced his way around the boundaries of the future lot. The fir trees still standing, seemed to shudder in anticipation, and as we stood at a safe distance, Kevin threw in a firecracker. We could hear the apocalyptic roar of destruction, and as we peeled away on our bikes, a pillar of fire rose up into the evening sky like an angry genie. At last we flopped, exhilarated behind a copse of trees from a safe distance and witnessed our brief foray into life without rules. Eden was in flames. The sirens wailed past us in the evening air, as the appropriate authorities arrived at our scene of willful destruction. Not one of us even remembered the promise of cash, but it was worth it.

6

~

Oscar

That night in the pup tent I tossed and turned, as a strange recurring dream returned to my brain. I don't know why I dreamed about Oscar. Oscar was a fish in the pet store downtown. Sometimes when we were bored, we would stop by at noon on a Saturday, the time when Oscar got his regular feeding. Oscar did not take regular fish food. Although clownish-looking and overly large, like a cartoon caricature, Oscar was a prized exotic fish, named after his breed, and a carnivore. His lunch every day was culled from the stock of lesser fish, like guppies and goldfish. Oscar would hover in his tank, his round eyeball almost pressed against the glass as he waited in anticipation for the "plop."

In my dream, Ned the owner dropped in a hapless mid-sized orange goldfish, which immediately dashed to the furthest corner of the tank, trying to cram itself in the small enclosure afforded by the plastic castle nestled there. While the cheerful flow of bubbles streamed optimistically to the surface of the tank, Oscar did nothing except to station himself comfortably in the water, and the only perceptible movement was in the eyeball which was on the same side as the goldfish. Suddenly there was a flash of motion, Oscar disappeared and immediately reappeared in the same position where the goldfish had been. Some gravel and fish poop swirled around and settled again to the bottom of the tank. Oscar turned and looked me in the eye, savoring some kind of timeless primordial knowledge that I had only partially begun to decipher. In my dream, though I know it is not possible for a fish, Oscar smiled at me with the broadest of grins, and I immediately sat up awake, with the cold sweat sticking to my sleeping bag and my heart pounding in the semi-darkness. As the image of Oscar's strange fish-smile faded into the back of my mind, I suddenly felt very vulnerable.

7

~

The Mark of Adam

The next morning was Sunday, and as we entered the house we saw a pile of pancakes waiting, and Grandma in her pill-box hat and fur stole ready to head out the door. Sunday was what she called her 'special day,' and she would walk down to the Saint Barnabas Anglican Church where the bells were already calling out the new day, to meet her friend Emily. Their afternoon would promise a proper British tea, complete with a few stiff shots of Emily's home-made strawberry wine, after which they would watch the Lawrence Welk show together, feeling as fine and elegant as any of the ladies being whisked around the dance floor. "Sure you don't want to come with us?" my mother queried. "The holy rollers?" my Gran called out as she went out the door, "I would rather be caught *dead*"!

Ricky and Jimmy had been happily abandoned by their mothers, to the chance of some "free babysitting," and we suffered the incursions of Brylcreem and formal dress, while my mom clucked in pleasure about what a handsome bunch we were.

It was Pentecost Sunday, which is the ecclesial equivalent for Pentecostals, of Saint Patrick's Day for the Irish. We crowded in one of the last rows, itching and squirming. I watched a small boy in front of me who was holding a coloring sheet from Sunday school which showed a church with a tall steeple, a smiling sun, and a silhouette of a dove, descending downwards. The upper corner was adorned with the title "Holy Spirit." The small boy frowned for a moment, crossed out the words, and wrote beside them, "Dive Bomber" with an arrow pointing to the dove, and then added a trail of missiles raining down on the church. He turned and looked at me as if seeking a partner in crime, then screwed the end from the pen, tore a little piece from the corner of his drawing, and placed it in his mouth. Checking back to see if I was still watching, he took the spit wad out of his mouth and put it in the shaft of the pen. A few rows ahead of us, sat Bradley Milton. He was famous for his frizzy carrot-colored perm, a testimony from the men's salon to the wisdom of leaving well enough alone. The problem was that his hair was galvanized in a state of atrophy—dry, ample, and with the tendency to become charged with static electricity like a balloon that had been rubbed on a wool sweater. Sure enough, science ruled the day when the small boy blew the spit wad slightly off course, but the projectile, like a small planet orbiting a gravitational center, displayed a course-correct that would have done Galileo proud. The spit wad was sucked into the back of Bradley's hair as if by divine fiat. There it sat, lodged beside a few others, specks of manna in the otherwise barren wilderness. The small boy looked back at me and laughed.

We opened up with a popular hymn, "To Be Used of God" by Audrey Mieir. I had never quite caught the lyric, and the only thing I heard in my mind was "to be *USE*-ified," which sounded to me like just another part of the holy lexicon along with being justified, glorified and sanctified. God must surely have *use-ified* the Apostle Paul when he struck him down on the Damascus road and to me, getting *use-ified* sounded like the kind of thing that would leave you both holy *and* useful. I wondered if such an act of God would fix you for good, but the idea unsettled me because what if you still wanted a do-over?

All of this put me in mind of a conversation I once overheard where my Dad told my Mom that most members of the church were ossified, and she had asked in response whether or not he had ever read the story of Ezekiel and the valley of dry bones. I determined that being ossified and *use-ified* must be pretty much the same thing.

Not too far in front of us, opera man was gearing up into fine form. We called him opera man, because he broke out with the seismic volume of a Caruso whenever he sang, proud to stand out, but with little attention paid to the small matter of being in tune. Opera man was the musical equivalent to hitting a fly with a hammer and had been kicked out of the choir because he only ever intended to be a one-man-show. His ongoing revenge was his very affected and cacophonous harmonies, which were inflicted on the congregation, sneaked between stanzas for emphasis, and always building to a dramatic crescendo, which soared over and beyond the end of the song. We giggled and watched as people turned and ribbed each other, winking and smiling at one of the most timeless forms of human comedy—the sometimes considerable distance between how we see ourselves, and how we are perceived by others.

Up on the stage our reverend, Pastor Winters welcomed the crowd and invited us to turn to the third chapter of Genesis. I opened my King James Bible and followed as he read:

> "And the eyes of them both were opened, and they knew that they were naked; and they sewed fig leaves together and made themselves aprons. And they heard the voice of the LORD God walking in the garden in the cool of the day: and Adam and his wife hid themselves from the presence of the LORD God amongst the trees of the garden
>
> And the LORD God called unto Adam, and said unto him, Where art thou?
>
> And he said, I heard thy voice in the garden, and I was afraid, because I was naked; and I hid myself. And he said, who told thee that thou wast naked"?
> (GENESIS 3:7–11 KJV)

This last sentence, he turned and thundered to the congregation, for emphasis.

Now, *naked* is a word you don't often hear in church, and it was having its effect on Ricky. I turned and noted that he was already breaking a sweat, no doubt thinking about our neighbor and wondering how the reverend could peer into the machinations of his guilty conscience, with such x-ray precision.

"*Original sin*," the Pastor Winters proclaimed pointedly, thumping his Bible for emphasis. "Its mark is on us all. The mark of *Adam*," he cautioned, his hand sweeping out over the congregation, as he revved into high gear.

After the sermon, Ricky, Jimmy, Kevin and I reconvened in my tree house and compared religious notes. Jimmy went to the United Church, which my mother had caustically noted, was not much more than Liberals at prayer. Ricky was a Roman Catholic and had recently been confirmed, something that he took as a personal accomplishment. Kevin did not go to church at all and was proud of it. Ricky was telling us about the Catholic Eucharist. "And it turns into the real and actual blood of Jesus," he informed us. "It has, like magical powers. If you take Eucharist every week, you can get to do the *regular* sins, and they don't even count." Kevin seemed to ponder this for a brief moment, then punched Ricky in the arm. "What's *that* for?" he asked, looking aggrieved. "For being an idiot." Kevin noted disdainfully. "You know what?" he said. "I bet if you punched Jesus in the arm, he wouldn't do anything about it even though he could totally miracle your ass if he wanted to. That's boring. Superman would punch you out in a second if you tried to mess with him. He is tough. You know who I would like to have been? I would like to have been a *Nazi*." At this dark pronouncement, he paused for dramatic effect, and continued. "What's the point of all those World War Two guys dying to save *other* people? The Nazis just took what they wanted. They got free girlfriends, money, cars, and all kinds of stuff, just because the other people were too wussy to stop them. What's the point of being good, or even lucky, if you could be *tough* instead"? We looked at each other, momentarily weighing his logic.

Kevin had to leave for his weekend job, working on a pig farm. He hated it because the ammonia-like stench of pig manure invaded his pores so deeply that the strongest soap could not wash it out for days afterwards. Girls at school would sometimes giggle about it on a Monday and snort pointedly while passing him in the hallway. This repeated humiliation fostered in him, a deep hatred of animals that he would privately vent as opportunity arose.

"I dare you guys," he said. There is a tent revival meeting tonight by Whaley's Corners, and I am going to set off my biggest roman candle, in the middle of the service. "I bet," he said, as if in a taunt, "that you guys are too chicken to show your sorry faces. It's going to be *good*," he beamed.

8

~

The Pastor's Dilemma

Pastor Winters had a dilemma. He was preaching to the choir—literally, and this was a problem. The church needed some new converts. Now the Pentecostals may be famous for speaking in tongues, but like all self-respecting protestant churches, their overall emphasis was to add to the roll call of the elect. That meant that on most Sundays, the service devolved into a bit of prolonged hectoring for the same group of people to come forward and receive Jesus as their personal savior all over again just in case the last time didn't catch. Now by twelve noon what most people truly had on their minds was pot roast and what they were going to do in the lazy hours after church, but it seemed that a quorum of the repentant must be reached at the altar, before all could escape out the front door.

The previous Sunday particularly weighed on the reverend's mind like a portent of ill fortune. Bill Foster was a former bad-boy who had recently got saved and married into one of the more prominent families of the parish. He was enjoying his newfound fame by occasionally singing in church, after which as a bonus venue, he would give his personal testimony. The problem is that telling the same old story risked losing your audience—unless you could come up with some newer and more savory sins, and this is what Bill did. He recreated the dynamic—the dangerous leanings of his soul toward the licking flames of hell, his moment of epiphany, and his personal euphoria when he turned to Jesus—all over again.

The problem was that Bill had failed to properly calculate his audience. The somewhat new machinations of the Hippie movement meant that the congregation was enamored of the more unfamiliar and exotic sins, like getting 'on drugs.' If Jesus could save you from drugs, you had a great testimony.

But Bill's tales of perdition would get taller, as he salted his testimony for good measure, with a sprinkle of petty larceny, and recent marital infidelities. The reverend was troubled because he had noted Bill's young wife weeping in the front row, and not for joy. He had also had a terse benediction tossed in his general direction by Bill's mother-in-law as she stormed out the door. "*Jesus* may forgive him, but not before *I* lay hands on him," she had prophesied. Reverend Winters had a dark vision of what happens to a church that drinks its own bathwater, and he knew that he needed a revival. He had to either get some new converts or get the old ones more saved than they already were.

Accordingly, he had invited in a guest speaker whose ticket was that he would discern and cast out demons, and do some faith healing for good measure, the Apostle Everglad. Like a visiting circus, the tent had been raised on the edge of town, a local gospel quartet had been sourced as the entertainment, and so far, it promised all the makings of a good revival. He had sensed the pleasure across the faces of his somewhat bored Sunday charges, and he was glad and optimistic. And tonight, he didn't have to preach himself. Reverend Winters sat and drank his tea that afternoon with the relief of a struggling husband who gives up the wrench and calls in a professional plumber. This toilet was about to get a serious Roto-Rooting.

Seven PM rolled around. Apostle Everglad checked his somewhat orange makeup in the mirror and tightened the knot in his tie. On the other side behind the makeshift stage and sound equipment, the crimson carpets sat waiting on the grass for the knees of the newly repentant, and the Apostle gargled, finding his voice in good form. The crowd was starting to arrive. Gospel muzak, electricity and repentance were in the air.

Outside, Ricky, Jimmy, Kevin and I edged toward the far periphery of action, back beyond the rows of collapsible chairs, and found in the darkness behind the cables and boxes, a vantage point from which to watch. Kevin as planned, had come equipped with a small cardboard carton filled with some very promising-looking incendiary devices and a pack of matches.

9

~

The Apostle

Floyd Fulton had been an awkward teen whose vector in life had been in question for a while. His father, sprung from generations of farmers, chaffed at his unwillingness to awake at the crack of dawn and do chores. Floyd had drifted through his teens on autopilot, at best. The day his life changed had been when he met Bernetta, a preacher's daughter who was divinely appointed in all the right places. Floyd had been smitten from the first day when she stuck her tongue down his throat, and after a few weeks of various stages of undress in the back of his father's car by the river road, Bernetta had given him some advice. "Floyd," she said, "I am a preacher's daughter. You have to talk to my Dad." Bernetta's father was a former Fuller Brush man before he had become a preacher and had quickly learned the ropes of selling in the toughest bare-knuckle arena of them all, door-to-door sales to housewives. He knew people and when he looked at Floyd, he saw a glimmer of promise. "What are you planning to do, son" he queried Floyd, who was perched nervously on the edge of the living room couch sporting a somewhat forlorn-looking clip-on tie? "Sir," stuttered Floyd. You know that Leafs defenseman Tim Horton? He is offering franchises in his doughnut chain, and my Dad has offered to loan me the money." "*Doughnuts*," scoffed Bernetta's father, "don't you know there's no money in doughnuts? Son, if you like, I can take you into the family business. Have you ever considered *religion*"?

Religion it turned out, worked rather well for Floyd. Not only did it allow you to sleep in, the job was varied, involved the bonus of travel, and it turns out he would enter the family business with the best assets a Pentecostal Evangelist could ask for—a resonant voice, good hair that responded well to aerosol spray, and a smoking hot wife. The only thing that he did was to tweak his own lackluster past by changing his moniker, and he chose a new title that promised a little more allure—The Apostle Everglad.

His father-in-law's advice echoed in his ears as he adjusted his Elvis-white blazer with exaggerated lapels. "Son," he had offered, "you know why a grocer never runs out of work"? "No," responded Floyd. "It's because people gotta eat," he said. "Your market is assured. You know why a preacher never runs out of work?" he continued. Floyd scratched his head. "It's because son, people gotta *sin*"!

He had slapped Floyd on the back, infused with the gusto of experience.

10

~

Tent Meeting

The Apostle Everglad had a secret. He was a problem gambler. Everglad nursed a private penchant for games, which promised the thrill of high stakes. Believing that his spiritual fortunes were on the rise, he decided to give the favor of God a little push, in the form of a few high-risk card games, played in sequestered locations and guarded by unsavory-looking doormen. But God had been strangely silent as of late, and the Apostle had compromised his family domicile with a promissory note that had to be dealt with before his wife and father-in-law found out. Looking out over the crowds rolling in, he breathed an optimistic sigh, sensing that his moment of destiny was only a matter of reaching out to grasp it.

The visiting gospel group dove into a snappy version of Isaac Watt's "At the Cross" in four-part harmonies, and the ten-foot-high cross, decorated with Christmas lights, was switched on to great effect. Everglad strode up to the microphone, opened up his Bible to the book of Matthew and faced the crowd.

"What went ye out into the wilderness to see? A reed shaken with the wind? . . . A man clothed in soft raiment? Behold, they that wear soft clothing are in kings' houses. But what went ye out for

to see? A prophet? Yea, I say unto you, and more than a prophet." (MATTHEW 11:7–9 KJV) He looked up and paused, as if to indicate himself.

"*Seed faith*! Do you have enough faith to plant a seed? Plant a seed and it will grow. Tell me, did you come here today expecting a miracle? A Holy Ghost infusion in your finances? Tell the rent bill "don't come today." Did you come for a healing? Tell the doctor, '*stay at home!*' The *Great Physician* is here. He is moving amongst you," he intoned, his voice quieting down to an affecting hush.

"*Holy Ghost power*," he whispered. "Can you say it? "*Holy Ghost power*," echoed the crowd, beginning to stir with excitement. "That's right," continued the evangelist, "speak your words into being—the power of intent. Your words have *Holy Ghost power* here tonight. *Je-e-e-esus* is waiting just for you to reach out and touch the hem of his garment as he passes by."

The choir, as if on cue, jumped into a neat and harmonious version of "Pass me not, oh Gentle Savior" in the background. People looked around like spectators at a séance, who have been informed that the spirits are among them. An expectant hush fell over the audience as people started to sway to the music and raise their arms in the air.

The reverend crouched down and started to pace the stage, sweeping his hand out over the audience dramatically. "*Je-e-e-esus* is going to give the Devil a *black eye* here tonight" the Apostle shouted, sweat beginning to bead on his makeup. "*Do you believe it*"? He held out his microphone to the crowd. "*We believe*" they responded in unison.

"Then come on down to claim your miracle"! the Apostle erupted, beckoning with his hands, "*Jesus* is going to meet you here today." As the crowd advanced, one figure strode forward ahead of the others with a litheness that belied his advancing years. It was Moses, and he did not look to be in a good temper. "*Charlatan*" he roared, his boney finger extended in accusation, *"thief. . . robber. . . miscreant."*

The Apostle had some experience deflecting hecklers and his first instinct was to turn the dynamics around. *"Demon possessed,"* he called out with authority, hoping to grab the momentum before Moses got in too deep. "I discern a spirit of bitterness in this poor sinner coming forward, well the *Great Physician* is going to put the devil in a chokehold tonight. *Who wants to see it?"* he shouted out to the crowd. The white-haired martinet did not slow down his advance, and the apostle was beginning to feel more than a little apprehensive. Moses pulled back his arm with fist clenched, as he closed the gap between himself and the Apostle, who was frantically looking around for his deacons.

"Ushers, hold that man" the Apostle shouted. Two burly acolytes hastened forward looking like they meant business, and each grabbed the advancing geriatric by an arm. The apostle, sensing imminent victory, advanced on the scene, and the crowd fell back like spectators around a boxing match. *"Heal"* shouted the Apostle. *"Foul demon be gone"!* he cried as he open-palmed Moses on the forehead with a force that would have felled a lesser man.

The old man summoned his strength, and in a burst of action, shook off the two restrainers and clocked each in turn with a lightning-fast precision that showed the evidence of some practice as a pugilist. He turned his attention to the evangelist.

It was at that importune moment that Kevin sensed his moment of destiny and reached for the pack of matches. He chose the fattest of weapons from his arsenal, a four-inch thick beauty that but for the colored paper, looked like it could have been pulled from any theater of war. He lit the match, the fuse sputtered, and we all leaned back plugging our ears. The first volley burst forth with a whiz and a bang, over the heads of the crowd. The Apostle and Moses, grasping each other's lapels with fists pulled back, looked up in shock and holy terror as explosion after explosion of color burst forth over their heads.

"*Tongues of fire,*" shouted someone in the audience, pointing as another plume of colored flame erupted over the parishioner's heads. "It's the blessing of Pentecost," someone else yelled. Pandemonium broke loose as people began to fall like flies under the divine anointing, but it was unclear whether they were being slain in the Spirit, or simply ducking for cover. "*Shun-da-la doh-lan ya-con-doo-shah! Yah koon-dulu koodu-shah mak-kai*" a voice called out, bursting into heavenly tongues. "*Hallelujah*"!

After the meeting, the Apostle Everglad sat drinking a glass of cold water, as he mopped his brow and watched the satisfied crowds depart, still buzzing with versions of events that would feed the local gossip mill for weeks to come. "Hey Rev," said one of the deacons, "check this out, it was our best day ever." He raised one of the paper Kentucky Fried Chicken buckets, which were used to collect the offering, overflowing from the brim with crisp bills of generous denomination. "Sweet hour of prayer"! exclaimed the evangelist. "Well, Earl, let's hope they invite us back *next* year, praise God"!

"The Lord worketh in strange and mysterious ways," he intoned to himself in awe, looking into the quiet of the night and thinking of his promissory note.

II

~

An Armload of Potatoes

Alistair Moore studied his son carefully, looking for signs of deception. He was wondering if some of that canny Gaelic blood had passed on down as he looked into Kevin's eyes. School project? It sounded suspicious, but Kevin had persuaded him that his science class was studying astronomy and that he needed to be out after midnight on Friday in order to write an eyewitness account of the full lunar eclipse that would occur then. Alistair took another beer from the fridge, considering. A little lie here and there in life can get you far, he reasoned. To the victor went the prize, and prizes could be few and far between. So, he said yes, somehow tickled that his son at fourteen seemed to have more cojones than he had at the same age. Today's rule-breaker, tomorrow's CEO. He took another swig of his beer.

Kevin Moore was feeling invincible. His good luck streak seemed like it would never end. His current hijinks were mapped out, and he would need some good witnesses to uphold his reputation at school. He thought of Jimmy, Jacob and Ricky and reveled at the God-like status he had won after his stunt at the tent meeting. All it took was a bit of balls. He envisioned himself a conquistador, breaking down the barriers of society that seemed to keep the dupes of the civilized world trapped in endless cycles of boredom. His life was going to be anything but boring, he determined.

A lunar eclipse was a good time to pull any kind of prank because local authorities would already be busy. He had heard that any kind of lunar event brought out the loony tunes; it was statistical fact. Hospital wards and the police station filled up equally whenever there was a full moon.

He looked at his weaponry, imagining the possibilities that accompanied a good forty-pound bag of PEI red-skinned potatoes, and smiled. Jimmy, Ricky and I got permission once more to sleep outside in our pup tents, so we could be out too. "If I'm the brains, then you losers have to be my grunts," Kevin pronounced smugly. "That means, you gotta hoof my potatoes. . . *kapeesh*"? We each gathered as many as our knapsacks could carry and walked in a laden procession like the seven dwarves following Snow White up the hill, while the moon rose overhead. Competence Road was in that juncture where the farms ended, and the woods started, and all along to the left of the road, the creek snaked by. If anyone chased us, we could easily disappear, and not many people were of the mind to chase you too far and leave their car unattended on a hill. Kevin relished the success of the tent meeting fiasco in his mind, deciding that the best way to celebrate one triumph was on the cusp of the next.

Up in the sky, the moon presented itself as an unwieldy oversized orb, throbbing blood red. We sat in the dark, in an enclosure afforded by some cedar branches, and waited for a car to come down the hill. Kevin was unit commander. "Target approaching three-o'clock," he sang out, "*company prime your weapons*, wait 'till you see the whites of their eyes. . . ready, aim, hold. . . hold. . .. hold. . .. *fire*"! "Whump, boom, *splat*." Our first volley of missiles was fired off to great success. The car sped off and careened and wove its way, shaken, down the hill. Another car came up the rise, to the same end. One businessman in a suit leaped out of his car and chased us down the banks of the creek, which we forded with a nimble bound. For a moment he pivoted awkwardly in his dress shoes, on a smooth stone, then shook his fist and cursed at us before turning around in retreat.

We were having so much fun that soon we were running out of ammo. The contents of our bags came to an end as a red car with jacked up wheels and no hubcaps went up the hill and we landed a volley of potatoes that bounced off the front windshield. One rather large potato dented the car on the passenger side. The car sped up the hill and disappeared over the peak.

Kevin, without pausing ran out on the road, and stood there gathering potatoes in his arms. Eschewing the broken pieces, he untucked his shirt and collected as many whole potatoes as he could find, in the makeshift pouch. Just then headlights crowned the top of the hill, signaling the coming of more traffic from the opposite direction. The car peaked the hill, driving very slowly, and me, Jimmy and Ricky held our breath from the bushes when we saw that it was the red car we had just hit. Kevin did not notice at all, he was absorbed in his collections on the side of the road, unperturbed.

There is a saying that bad luck comes in threes, but I think I amended the number that day to two, when I saw Len and Gord Smith step out of the vehicle. They were twins in the senior grade, and they had a physical heft and perpetual five-o'clock shadow that made them look like ex-cons impersonating high school students. Len was captain of the football team, and Gord was captain of the Judo team. They were a daunting duo even when they were *not* mad.

Len Smith tapped Kevin on the shoulder, and he glanced up as if annoyed. "Hey kid," Len said, his face lit up like a ghoul in the spotlight of the car beams. "I think you *missed* one." He handed him a potato. Kevin's stared back in mute confusion. He stood up, fumbled with his bundle of potatoes, and stepped back, gape-jawed. "Did you by any chance throw potatoes at *my* car?" Gord inquired in a calm and deliberate voice. "No Sir, it wasn't me, *honest*," Kevin protested, while attempting in a panic to move his cache of potatoes around and out of view. "You mean this dint in my door did *not* come from you?" Len asked, pointing. He crossed his arms so that the ripples on his biceps made him look like Mr. Clean on steroids. Kevin stood trapped in the bright light of the car beams as we witnessed first-hand what 'deer caught in the headlights' looks like. Whether it was the anomaly of a lunar eclipse, or just the law of averages, it seems that Kevin's life was destined to become even more lively than he had planned. When Len's big ham fist met his face, he flew up in the air like a raptured soul, and landed on the other side of the road, leaving one of his running shoes still tied, in the middle. As Len and Gord got in their car and drove away, I made a mental note to self, that when standing in front of the judge, the search for a viable alibi is best not attempted while hiding an armload of potatoes.

12

~

Six Feet of Black Dirt

Ricky, Jimmy and I decided that it was time to delve into the mystery of Moses. We knew his farm because we passed by it often going up into the woods. It sported a dilapidated wooden barn to the left, and a brand-new aluminum red barn, to the right. The Northeys were known in the district for their strawberry operation and their property had a sign on the road, which proclaimed, "*Whatsoever a man soweth, that also shall he reap* (GALATIANS 6:7 KJV),*" and underneath that a space, then another smaller sign tacked on which was perhaps an afterthought, "*Shotgun loaded with rock salt*." We knew people who had picked at the Northeys, one had been found padding his strawberry flats with soil at the bottom and was handed directly over to the local constabulary. The Northeys were no-nonsense Baptists who had a judicious eye for business and their farm was prospering.

Sometimes in the late spring when we knew the Northeys were out in the fields, we would enter their abandoned wooden barn, climb up into the haymow, and jump down onto the ancient spongy pile of cow manure accumulating moss at the foot of the barn. It was about a thirty-foot drop, and it promised not much more than a momentary thrill, then the air knocked out of you like you got hit by a truck once you hit the bottom. We did it because it seemed like a tough thing to do, and it tickled our fancy in a perverse way. "Geronimo"! crowed Jimmy as he jumped, "Look out cow flops, here I come"!

That Monday afternoon, we crossed over the stone fence, threw a few crab apples at his cows for good measure, and spied with our scout binoculars, looking to see if we could find evidence of Moses and his shotgun. The trucks were gone so we didn't know if anyone was home. Soon a figure emerged from the farmhouse, it was Moses in bib overalls, carrying a large piece of lumber. He went into the abandoned wooden barn, as we followed from a safe distance. Finally, we reached the back of the barn, crept in by the back door, which was open a crack, and climbed up a wooden ladder to a loft up above where hay was stored. We peered over the edge in unison. Moses was bent over an ancient carpentry bench, an array of wooden planes sat on a shelf beside him. He was planing the board, deeply engrossed, his beard hanging down over the board as he grunted in rhythm with the action. Beside him stood what looked like a writing desk, nearly finished but lacking a top. As he planed, he rambled scripture to himself, "*Thus saith the Lord; Thou hast broken the yokes of wood; but thou shalt make for them yokes of iron.*" (JEREMIAH 28:13 KJV)" He planed for a bit, the thin shavings rising up in translucent curls, which he periodically brushed to the side as he worked. Moses stopped to caress the top of the board, checking for high points. He clucked his tongue, fingering a small portion of tear-out where the plane had caught a piece of cross-grain. He continued talking to himself, mumbling. "You son of a bitch, I should tear you down and rebuild you from scratch. The problem is if I did you over again perfect I might not like you as much as the first time. That's our dilemma," he mused.

Then the unimaginable happened. The board that was supporting me creaked, gave way in a cloud of dust, and I tumbled down to the ground at Moses' feet. I could hear Ricky and Jimmy yell, and I saw a blur of color as they both double-timed it out the door. I could smell the dank aroma of old manure, decaying barn wood, and musty hay filling my nostrils. Moses loomed over me as a dark silhouette, before he yanked me to my feet with an iron grip.

I did not expect what happened next. He thrust a wooden object into my hands and said gruffly "*Read it.*" I looked. It was an ancient molding plane, the color of old tea, and glossy to the touch from much handling. "*Read it,*" he grunted again. I gazed down at the plane. "What do you see?" he demanded. "I don't know," I stammered. "The *names*" he said, gesturing. I looked on the end of the plane and read stamped in the wood. "B. COOPER" in rough capital letters. "*And,*" he said. I looked again. There was another name under that, more faint. "R. KENNEDY." "And after that" he demanded. I saw another stamp, fainter than the first two, almost worn off. I held it up to the light. "T. SMYTHE." "You know what you are holding son," he asked. I looked at him puzzled. "*Dead men,*" he responded, "Those are the names of dead men, all in a line one after the other. They thought that the tool was something in their life, but they were wrong. They were something in the tool's life. The tool has outlasted them. "You know the problem with *people*"? He spit this last word out like an epithet. "They don't know what they're good for. Now this tool, is designed for something proper, and it honors its maker, and its purpose. You can't hammer with a saw and you can't saw with a hammer. The biggest problem with people, is that they get to choose. They don't know what they're *good for,*" he huffed, "that's where all the *trouble* comes from."

He beckoned me to the bench and pointed at the piece of wood. "It's *natural,*" Moses growled. When I work it, it tells me if I am doing a good or bad job. If I try to work against the way that wood is built, I won't get far. It's written in the grain. Looky here. Did you ever see anything looks like that? This is spalted maple. You know what that means"?

I looked back, mute. "Don't teach you much in school, do they son," he commented. This here wood, you know what it's doing? It's busy *dying*. That's right. Spalted maple is wood that has done gone half-rotten but ain't finished yet. All them black squig-gly lines and patterns and shapes, they are talking about a great war. When this wood starts to rot, the microscopic bacteria of the plant world, they gang up and try to take over. They's always two sides. When they can't figure out who is going to win, they carve up the face of this wood. One color is one bacteria. The other color is the other bacteria. Them black lines in the middle, that wiggle and swirl all over this board, they are battle lines. This wood is the story of nature in conflict. Always two sides trying to carve up the host. But, look at it. It is beautiful yet as it decays—there is still a divine artistry at work within it. We're all in a war, all them that's going to rot. And that would be you and me and all else that's walk-ing about on two legs living and breathing."

"You know who's the one going to win in the end?" he asked. "*Six feet o' black dirt* like you just fell on." I turned and fled from the barn, racing for home.

13

~

The Funeral

I was thinking of my Dad's funeral. It felt like an uncomfortable and unfamiliar combination of a dream and getting kicked in the gut, all at once. We walked like sleepwalkers through the established routine, cued and encouraged by a coterie of men in black suits from the funeral establishment. I stood awkwardly in the chapel as people commiserated while picking at the pinwheel sandwiches. My mother, in a black veil, was hugged by various parties around the room, some who were familiar to me, and others who were not. I felt the air was lead on my chest, the suffocating combination of artificial refrigeration and confined flowers cut off in mid-bloom. My hair was slicked back and an old lady with a pincushion hat and brown teeth bent down and breathed into my face with a Scottish lilt. "My, oh my, aren't you just like him though"? She pinched my cheek. "Now what are you and your mom going to do with yourselves," she wondered out loud. "All alone in the world, now isn't *that* a cruel thing"?

I knew we were all going to go home after that. It is just that home, now held a totally new meaning for me, I knew where our house was, but I didn't know the place in the world where home lived. I thought about my Dad. His own father had taken off with a younger woman, leaving Grandma abandoned to the world. My Dad was offered a job on the recommendation of his shop teacher, as the high-school maintenance man, and seeing his mother's predicament he took the position. It was this predisposition to help that made home seem like a safe place. My Dad had not lived for himself. He did not have the chance. I sat and thought about all the things that my Dad was and would never get to be. Everything he did in his life, risked vanishing from view as life inevitably marched on. What I was most afraid of, was that if I forgot my Dad, my life would somehow end before it even got started, but I didn't know why.

That night after my mom fell into bed with a widow's exhaustion, Grandma crept into my room and laid the cool, parchment-like skin on the back of her hand, on my wet cheek. "Jacob," she said, checking if I was awake. "Do you know what your Dad did in life? "Yes," I replied, "he fixed things." "Yes" said Grandma, "that was his job, but it also seems to have been his lot in life, to clean up messes and fix the broken things left behind by others. So, what he did, was very important and I want you to know that. In life, we are presented with things we can choose, and things we inherit. There are always those things left behind that we can fix or run off and leave broken. Now I don't want you to worry. Your Dad left us provided for, with an insurance policy so that the bills will continue to get paid. You know, what your Dad did was important. He provided, for me and for you. You would have had to experience the opposite arrangement to fully understand what that means. At a certain point, a man has to choose whether he would like to have firm principles, or a firm piece of the pie. Thank God your Dad had firm principles because there are plenty of folk out there who would choose the other." Grandma continued, "Jacob, you know my rassling? What gets me going is that the cheaters always seem to sneak by when the ref isn't looking. We are left to judge as spectators. That is why I hiss and boo so. But you know what? The people who keep on playing the game, show us something important—that what we do in the world, both good and evil, matters very much. That is why memory is so important. I know they say, 'forgive and forget,' but that is little better than treacle. It is easy to forget. That is a job for the careless of the world. Good people both forgive and remember. It is only holding the ache of wrong in your heart which can set the world aright again. Your Dad was dealt a certain hand of cards, and he did his best. In a world where the ref is looking the other way, most people choose to slide by with the easy choices. The *something* that your Dad did far outweighs the *nothing* that many people choose to do. Don't ever forget that. I want you to remember your Dad. Remembering will save you, and the world a heap o' trouble."

14

~

Gopher Guts

I was disappointed that Jimmy and Ricky had bailed on me. Nobody expected any valor from Ricky, but Jimmy was supposed to be my best friend. What if Moses had killed me? At school the next day, I eyeballed Jimmy when he slunk up beside me in the hallway. "Judas" I said to him. "Traitor"! "Aw c'mon, tell me, what did Moses do to you? How did you get away" Jimmy begged? "If it was me, I would've kicked that creepy old bastard in the nuts and run." "Yeah?" I replied. "I didn't see you there when the chips were down, did I? I think you and Ricky were out somewhere doing the chicken Olympics while I was fighting Moses. You know how I got away? I arm-wrestled Moses for my life, and I won. How about that?" I replied sarcastically. This last bit was meant to rankle Jimmy. Even though Jimmy had a big mouth, I was still stronger than him. I could beat him in an arm wrestle and it bothered him to no end.

Jimmy and I went a long way back, since the first time we spied each other over the fence that separated our yards. There was always a bit of rivalry between us, but we liked the same stuff. From early on, the thing that tied us together was the creek, which ran all the way from up in the woods by Moses' farm, past the school, and on down to the river. It was buried in some portions under the streets, as a long cavernous underground waterway that tied into the sewer systems and storm drains, a long tube of corrugated metal that eventually emptied into the river. We had discovered we could get in at one end, from a twist in the bars that we could slip through, and that is what we did. The next day we came back equipped with flashlights and high rubber boots, to transverse its length. We felt like the explorers who had found Doctor Livingston, brimming with accomplishment when we reached the other end, and after that it became one of our haunts for the summer. My mother always threatened she would wear me out with a switch if she heard we had been in it. "Boys," she cautioned, "what if there was a flash flood? That creek gets high pretty fast. I've even seen it overflowing onto the road more than once. If it started raining while you were underground, that tunnel would fill to the top pretty fast and you would be drowned." But that did not deter us.

We showed Ricky the next week. The three of us came equipped with flashlights and pails, determined to crawl the length of the storm drains and see where they went. We tunneled up, all in a row on our hands and knees, crawling as the spaces became more confined. At one point an enormous muskrat, oily looking and black silently slicked past us in the dark as we pressed our bodies up against the cement in disgust. Periodically, the tunnel would open out at a storm drain, which would give us the opportunity to stretch our legs and climb up the metal rungs to peer out from the grate and try to locate exactly where we were. At one point, I tied a red bandana around the grate, so we could discover it from the outside later on, scouting out the spot on our bikes. We found the red bandana after following a rough idea of our trajectory, all the way up to the top of Roland Drive, where it hit Competence Road and all the farms began. We had travelled over a mile underground. It tickled us because in our adolescent minds, we were in a dark subterranean world where none of the regular rules applied. It was like visiting Superman's Bizarro planet, the one that was a kind of mirror to the regular world of the good and unsuspecting citizens, only everything there was dark, opposite and contrary.

The other thing that we discovered in those sewer networks, was that the storm drains contained large fish, which had somehow become trapped. There they grew, and we would bring them out, with sloshing pails and sell them for twenty-five cents each to Mr. Lee who owned the all-you-can-eat-diner down by the river. We told him that the fish were from the sewer systems. "Don't matter" he snorted. "Canadians, they eat *anything* deep-fried in batter." At this he laughed and carried the fish into his restaurant.

The creek also housed an abundance of crayfish. One of our main entertainments was crayfish roulette. We would turn over rocks, reach down and snatch them between our fingers as their slimy grey claws clenched and their tails flipped in protest. When we got a bucketful, we would go up to the edge of Maranatha Boulevard and set the crayfish loose out onto the road, clumsy and scurrying blind in all directions. As the cars zoomed past, you would hear a periodic "crunch" when one of the wheels would flatten a crayfish and from our vantage point on the side of the road, we would squirm in disgust and delight.

The creek was also the place where I discovered that Jimmy and I were different. One day we were down there with our pails, and Jimmy's black lab, Duke. We had found a gopher hole and were determined to catch the gopher. Anybody knows that a gopher hole has not only an entry, but a secret exit on the other side, from which to escape. Duke had chased the gopher into the hole and was barking furiously at the portal. We decided to give Duke a little help, so we emptied buckets of water one after another into the hole to flush the gopher out. Eventually, our strategy worked. From the far end that exited out by the creek, we saw a tiny form emerge and dart his head about in all directions. Duke fell upon the gopher before we could react, barking with excitement as we followed close behind. The gopher chattered and squeaked while Duke rolled and swung it about in the air, snarling, snapping and tearing with his teeth. In that moment of frenzy, Duke seemed more like wolf than dog. Finally, the squealing stopped, and Duke tossed the limp body to the ground. There was not much left of the gopher. One of its eyes was bitten clear through, and its neck was torn open. Pink intestines trailed out of its body, and one leg was twisted off to the side attached only by a ligature of pink skin and fur. As dark flecks of blood began to collect in the dirt, the gopher continued to spasm erratically with the one good leg. Duke nudged the gopher with his nose, then turned, looking up at me for approval, and suddenly licked me. I shuddered at the sight of blood on my arm, and quickly wiped it on my jeans. The gopher was the first real flesh-and-blood being to die before my eyes and seeing the blood somehow changed it all—it was not like the cray-fish. I thought about my Dad, and how his inclination was always to be kind. I could not remember him harming any living thing, ever.

Suddenly from the side, Jimmy brought the butt end of a large chunk of wood down on the gopher's head, smashing it so that the brains squished out like pink and grey Jell-O onto the grass. He kicked the flaccid corpse to the curb, and collared Duke. "C'mon boy, good dog. Let's go home."

On the way, Jimmy started to sing a Boy Scout camp song. "Great green globs of greasy, grimy gopher guts, mutilated monkey nuts, hairy pickled piggy feet, French fried eyeballs in a pan of bloody meat and me without my spoon. . ."

"I wonder what's for lunch," he mused aloud, almost as an afterthought.

15

~

Batman is Missing

In my dream, I am dressed in my green swimming trunks, my red jacket and a yellow towel tied around my neck. I have a large "R" cut out from construction paper and pinned to my left breast with an oversized safety pin, and I am peering out at the world from behind a black mask. I am Robin, the Boy Wonder, second only to Batman. I amble confidently out on the street and begin to walk the block in the hazy sun as the streets are illuminated with a faint pink glow that does not seem to be coming from anywhere in particular, like a Renoir painting. I welcome the stares of passersby and admirers like the elderly and infirm who need my protection. "Look, it's Robin, the Boy Wonder!" they call out, and wave. I salute the police officers, who honk their horns as they drive past. A few old ladies give me a deferential smile and I raise my hand, benevolent in my modesty. In the dream I arrive home, happy and proud. My mother is waiting at the door. She grabs my arm and shakes me. "*Where is Batman?*" she shouts, frantic. "*I don't know,*" I protest. In my self-absorption, I had forgotten all about Batman. "Where *is* he?" insists my mother, wringing my lapel and slapping my face until my head spins "Tell me where he is"! "I don't *know,*" I call out, and as I wake up, I realize I am crying.

16

~

The Other Side of the Fence

Jimmy had been getting on my nerves and I could not decide whether he was thick, or just secretly mean. My Dad was dead. Jimmy's on the other hand, was on the rise. He had inherited a small nest egg, and invested it in his own brokerage business, which meant two things—more cash, and more leisure time. People were working for him. Suddenly a new car appeared next door with power windows, the next week a brand-new canoe on roof racks. At every juncture Jimmy would crow and strut about what his Dad was doing, oblivious to my discomfort. "My Dad is a *boss* you know," he would chirp. "He gets to tell people what to do. Was *your* Dad ever a boss"?

Jimmy's Dad was a happy man. He laughed a lot. He particularly laughed at job interviews where he loved to put people on the spot. A very nervous girl in a knee-length plaid skirt and a buttoned-up white blouse had sat primly that day, answering an ad in the paper for a secretary. Jimmy's Dad questioned her; "Did you know that I am looking for a KBM," he asked. The girl looked puzzled. "KBM," he repeated. "Tell me, do you type"? "Very well," she said. "First in my class. I can type sixty words a minute." "Amazing," replied Jimmy's father. "Maybe you can be my new KBM. Keyboard Monkey, that's what it stands for. Have you ever heard of the Infinite Monkey Theory"? The girl looked both shocked and puzzled which was exactly the effect he was after. "The idea, is that if you had a million monkeys on a million typewriters you would eventually recreate the great literature of the universe from Shakespeare on down to the Bible all over again. Do you think you qualify"? The girl stammered and opened her mouth, not quite knowing what to answer. Jimmy's Dad burst out in raucous laughter, tickled beyond measure at his own cleverness. "I have just one more question," he said. "Tell me, if somebody dropped a quarter on the carpet, would you pick it up?" "Well, of course," beamed the girl, recovering, "who wouldn't"? "You're hired," said Jimmy's dad, smiling.

His brokerage business also made him happy. "There are buyers and there are sellers" he would say, "and there are only two things that matter, what you want to get paid for something, and what someone else is willing to pay. Value, now that is an illusion," he would laugh. "I just link people up, so they can get what they want. What it *costs* them is no matter to me. And you know the beauty of it all?" he would enquire of all those willing to listen, "I get paid, no matter what, it's *other* people who lose their money." Yes, Jimmy's Dad was a happy man indeed, one who knew the price of everything and the value of nothing.

Sometimes lost in my own thoughts I would wander to the other yard next door. Mrs. Anderson was a divorcée, and she had a set of six-year-old twins whom she had dubbed, "Double trouble" for the benefit of the neighbors. Sometimes when she felt particularly vexed, she would treat herself to an afternoon at the salon, at which time she would tie the twins to the swing set that she obliquely referred to as "my free babysitter." Strangely, everyone in the neighborhood would shore up this particular arrangement, as if all was right in the world and they would keep a watchful and approving eye, from a distance. Once Jimmy approached the twins as if to untie them. "Boy," called one of the other neighbors out cutting his grass. "What do you think you are doing? Do you want me to tell Mrs. Anderson"? Sometimes the boys *did* escape, and when they did, they would find some personal item of their mother's in the house, to either hide or destroy. After that they would bind themselves to the swing set once again, feeling very satisfied with themselves, and waiting eagerly for her to discover what item was missing or broken in a puzzled rage. I deliberated whether having two of them made their delinquent tendencies even worse. I pondered what would happen if one of the twins stopped being bad and decided suddenly one day to be good instead. It was something I had never considered, that a person might choose to be different from all those around him like a new Adam walking out alone into the world all over again, ditching Eve and making better choices.

I considered all the useless people that God had made in the world; the ones who seemed so very satisfied with themselves seemed to be in control and I wondered if that would ever change. I thought about my Dad and weighed him up against Jimmy's Dad. Jimmy's Dad did very little, in fact. His "work" was really, living from the efforts of others. He was not very much different from the long, slick and unsavory tapeworm that Jimmy's dog had coughed up last year, that had been hiding in his belly as a free rider. My Dad, I thought, had always had something useful to do. Unlike Jimmy's Dad, you could actually see and measure what he did, and realizing this made me feel better. I could see through Jimmy's kitchen window on the days that I felt like avoiding him, and watch his family at the table, laughing and talking. Jimmy would look at me sideway and pretend he did not notice me out in the yard. I think that what Jimmy really wanted was for me to feel jealous of him, and I could not for the life of me understand why.

It is hard to be on the outside of things. I knew that my situation in life was painfully different from Jimmy and his family, but I decided in the end, that it was something I would have chosen no matter what. It came down to what was better, to manage yourself wisely, or to manage others carelessly. It seemed to me that a man could be noble based on his choices alone if he really wanted to, and that was enough. It was a way of living that might even last longer in the end. That was how it was for those lone heroes on the TV westerns who died fighting the bad guys. It made their lives expand into something bigger even though they got killed. I also thought about people who seemed like they were big shots. Most of them had one thing in common. They were all wrapped up in themselves, bent on figuring out ways to get more important, buy more stuff, and boss more people around. If they died, their importance would come to a crashing end, and maybe after that, no one would really miss them at all. Whether or not my Dad had been important to anyone else, suddenly did not seem to matter very much. What really mattered, was that my dad had been important to *me*.

17

~

My House My Rules

It was a sunny day, a perfect day for bike riding. Roy's mom had brought home bright rainbow streamers for the handlebars, and a new horn with a rubber squeeze-ball that gave a satisfying duck-like 'honk' when you pressed it. Roy adorned his bike with these most recent of accoutrements and rode out proudly on display to the neighborhood with his streamers flowing behind in the breeze. He waved wildly at the passersby, honking his horn as he went, and some cars honked back. It was a good day, about as perfect as Roy could imagine. "Look at my bike" called Roy happily, "my *Mom* got it for me"! Roy was headed for Nando's Pizza at the local strip mall. It was one of his regular stops when he made his rounds, because Jenny the waitress would always give him a chocolate banana milkshake for free and it was his favorite kind.

Nando was from the Czech Republic. He had escaped into Austria during the Prague Spring of 1968, when the Soviet behemoth had flexed its muscle. He had a shaved head, with a forward slanting forehead adorned with a bushy eyebrow that extended from one side to the other without pause. He hated Communists with a passion, and was the proud proprietor of his establishment, in which a kitschy sign meant for housewives voiced his favorite mantra, "*My house, my rules.*" Pizza had been a default because Nando was disinterested in cooking, and pizza was easy. He would stand by the oven door, eyeballing his customers and enjoying the machinations of rule in his tiny kingdom. Jimmy and I arrived after school and Jimmy had contrived to play one of his favorite tricks.

One of the things Nando had done, was to spike his ancient juke box with a smattering of Moravian folk ballads for those moments when he was feeling nationalistic. When someone put in a nickel and punched "Yakety Yak" by the Coasters, or "In the Ghetto" by Elvis Presley, they would get Nando's music instead, by "accident." Nando would smile expansively at his customer, spread his hands out and pronounce, "Hey look at that, must be *broken*, huh?" and then burst into raucous laughter. Nando was the ideal candidate for any practical joke, because he was naturally paranoid from years of living under the duress of communist rule. His latent suspicion was about as safe as a tank of gasoline beside a lighted cigarette. What Jimmy liked to do was to stoke the jukebox with nickels, and choose one of Nando's planted 45's, to play over and over. The joke was that you could leave, and watch the fireworks from a safe distance, or simply imagine. The best part was that Nando would begin to sing along with a patriotic tear in his eye, all the while suspiciously eyeballing those non-fans of Moravian folk music amongst his customers, which included almost everybody. "*My house, my rules*" he would snort to himself, resentfully.

18

~

The Bigger Fish

Jimmy and I ordered a swamp water, our favorite drink. Swamp water was not really a flavor name, but the default for those who could not make a decision. It was a grey mixture of every stop on the soda fountain, the sum total of what it means to choose both everything and nothing at the same time. While Jenny was busy filling the glasses from the fountain, Jimmy slipped a stack of nickels into the jukebox, and selected a Moravian tune to play over and over. We sat to watch the fun. The song played once. Nando sang along robustly while rolling a pizza. The song played again. Nando started to scan his line of seated guests with a vague sense that he was being mocked. At that moment Roy burst in, grinning from ear to ear. "Look at my bike," he offered. "it's got new streamers, and a real horn. Wanna see"? "Sure Roy," Jimmy agreed. We stepped outside to offer some exaggerated and obsequious praise. "Oh *wow*, wish I had a bike like that" sang Jimmy, winking at me from the side. "My Mom got it for me. It's got *everything*," Roy chimed. Roy went back inside the store to enjoy his banana chocolate milkshake, and Moravian folk music blared forth when he opened the door. From inside behind the counter, Nando looked at the both of us doubtfully. Jimmy turned to me. "Let's take the air out of his tires," he said. "Then you'll see how much that simpleton likes his bike when he has to push it all the way home." Inside, the Moravian folk tune played for the third time as customers linked eyes uneasily and Nando's face began to turn a bright red.

"C'mon Jimmy let's get out of here," I said. "No" he insisted. If you are my friend you're going to watch me let the air out of his tires and you're not going to say a word about it. I don't know why Jenny gives that half-wit a free milkshake every single time he shows up. It only encourages him. Man, what a total *zero*"! I placed my hand on Jimmy's arm to restrain him as he bent down beside the bike and Jimmy looked up at me defiantly with anger starting to flare in his eyes. "You're such an ass hole" I said to him. Jimmy challenged back. "Hey, it's time to choose. It's either *me*, or the *retard*," he said. Inside, the same tune played over for the fourth time, and the door opened as another non-fan of Moravian folk music slipped out. "*Me—or—the—retard!*" repeated Jimmy, whispering and jabbing his finger into my chest for emphasis.

I think we had been pushing toward a skirmish for a long time, and that is what happened. I don't remember who grabbed who first, but soon we were rolling around on the ground grappling and pummeling with our fists. A voice suddenly rang out over both of our heads. "Well, well, look who we got here!" the voice crowed. "It's a two-for-one deal"! We looked up to see the silhouette of Bart Wilson looming over us, rubbing his palms together in satisfaction.

I am not sure if anybody inside the store knew what was happening outside, as the jukebox played the Moravian tune over for the fifth time. Bart meanwhile, had us pinned on the ground with the full weight of his knees jammed on our chests, as he brandished an overly large jackknife an inch over our faces. "I should cut out your eyeballs" he gloated. We'll see who pisses himself then. Where's your fat little friend, inside"?

Nando finally snapped as the Moravian folk tune played over for the sixth time. Had he escaped Czechoslovakia only to be taken for a fool? He grabbed his pepperoni cleaver from beside the wooden cutting board and headed out the door. We were on the ground contemplating our mortality, when suddenly Bart was yanked stiffly upward by the hair as if by a divine force not within our immediate periphery. The next thing we saw was Bart screaming and crying on his back, with Nando clutching him by the throat, and pounding his head on the ground, while swearing in Czech and waving the razor-sharp meat cleaver menacingly in the air. We had unknowingly witnessed a lesson that will come to all eventually—that in the great food chain of life, there will always be a bigger fish.

Jimmy and I hopped on our bikes and hustled home, not talking about our fight. We ended up lying on our stomachs, eating peanut butter sandwiches and enjoying a tacit truce brokered over our favorite afternoon matinée, Monster Movie. The creature from the Black Lagoon was lurking beneath the waters of the Amazon, as a shapely girl in a one-piece bathing suit swam unsuspecting up above. We shuddered in unison at his labored reptilian breathing as he inspected the comely silhouette gliding through the waves up above him and closed in. I bit into my peanut butter and took a sip from my can of root beer. I'm sure that what Jimmy and I temporarily shared was the almost palpable relief, which happens in that moment when someone *else* becomes the prey.

19

~

Checking the Fine Print

We spent a lot of time reading a pile of dog-eared comic books up in my tree house, mostly dreaming about all the offers in the back pages. Our favorite was the Charles Atlas ad, where the skinny guy gets muscles, saves the girl, and punches out the local tough. We tried hard to build ourselves up, using broomsticks with concrete-filled tomato juice cans affixed to the ends, but we still ended up looking like skinny Matt in the 'before' picture. Ricky laughed at us. "Man, you guys are dummies," he said. "Don't waste your time on that stuff, that's for amateurs. Me, I'm learning kung fu! It's pure science, the power of technique, undisputed. You can win *any* fight, no problem." The next day he brought over his mail order lesson plans, so we could all get a look. They were mini comic books with illustrated scenarios showing how a bully would come at you, and how you would fight back. The only problem was that Ricky confused contemplation of the thing, with mastery of the thing.

He was in stark contrast to Kevin, who was following the Charles Atlas workouts every morning for an hour and was already showing a hint of muscle. High noon arrived when he finally called out Ricky, who was bragging about how he was going to get a black belt in the mail. "Ok, tough guy," said Kevin. "If you're a kung fu master, prove it. Fight me then." They squared off in the middle of the yard and instantly Ricky started circling and dancing around Kevin, waving his arms about in the air in his best praying mantis pose and emitting cheesy sounds from his mouth like you might hear on a Friday night kung fu movie. To make matters worse, Ricky removed his belt, doubled it up and started to swing it around like it was a pair of nun chucks. Instead of being dazzled and intimidated by this intended display of prowess, Kevin stopped fighting, put his hands on his hips and started to laugh. "Kid" he said, "You're going to kung fu me with a *belt*"? Suddenly, Kevin made a feint to the right, and as Ricky ducked and covered, Kevin kicked him squarely in the nuts. Ricky fell down squirming and crying and gasping for air. "What was that?" he protested, cradling his jewels and moaning in pain. "Hey numb-nuts," said Kevin as he helped him up, "that was *my* kung fu lesson. Never leave your balls exposed. No charge. The entertainment alone was worth the price of admission." He walked away smirking to himself.

Ricky came back the next month, with a brown paper bag, well creased from opening and closing, and bursting forth with a collection of coupons cut from the back of cereal boxes. After the failed kung fu lessons, his sanguine pursuit of items that promised to be nearly free, was simply diverted to a new scheme. His favorite rumination involved how slick his life would be, and how amazed his friends would be when they saw what he was going to get this time around. Forget the X-Ray Specs and the Sea Monkeys, those were for babies. The item he most coveted, was the Plutonium Submarine, over seven feet long with rockets that fired, and a real periscope. A real live submarine for kids! Man, his friends would be *so* jealous. Ricky heard from his cousin, that *his* friend was related to the kid in the States who had saved up all his coupons for an entire year and sent away for the Plutonium submarine. When it arrived (he was told) a police car with sirens escorted it suspended on the back of a large truck, which unloaded the submarine onto the kid's front lawn while the neighbors gawked and exclaimed. He got his picture in the newspaper and *everything* (or so he was told). Ricky had saved up pop bottles for a whole month to cover the seventy-five cent pre-paid shipping fee and prayed to the glow statue of Mary over his bed almost every night, to ensure that they would make no mistake in his address. He contemplated his mother's dire prognostications about those who wish and gloated privately over the iron-clad guarantee—"*Made from sturdy two-hundred-pound test material. If you don't think it is the greatest toy you ever had—just send it back for a full refund,*" the ad had promised. Ricky mailed off his coupons and waited. It would be so slick. Jimmy and Jacob were always calling him a doofus and it was the image of their dazzled countenances that he entertained most frequently as he drifted off to sleep.

"Ricky, you got a package in the mail," called out his mom one day after school. Ricky rushed out, to find his mom clutching a long irregular shaped parcel, wrapped in brown paper and tied with string. "Plutonium Submarine," read the stamp on the side of the brown paper. Ricky's heart fell. What he found inside the wrapper was indeed a seven-foot long submarine, but it was one that was to be had only after folding up a large bundle of somewhat dilapidated-looking printed cardboard components according to the manufacturer's instructions.

"A *paper* submarine," whined Ricky. "What good is *that* in the water"?

"Ahhh, the large print giveth, but the small print taketh away"! hooted his father sagely from the side of the yard, trimming a hedge. "Wish in one hand and piss in the other and see which gets full first!" echoed his mother, feeling very smug indeed.

20

~

The Flood

They say that lightning never strikes in the same place, twice. I have always taken that saying to mean that basic mathematics and the laws of probability should work against bad luck. Those who say that have never seen a real rainstorm.

Boom! The thunder crashed as the sky lit up with natures' own fireworks. The rain came down in torrents, ran in tiny rivulets into gullies, crevices and cracks, found weak points of entry, and gathered its own force as every rivulet whispering together pushed and jostled to make their way to the great river at the bottom of the hill. On their journey, they carried with them the grey dust and the seeds of the earth, like so much flotsam and jetsam in the mud. The creek was high, surging beyond its banks onto the road and like any normal kids, there we were right in the middle of it, watching and exclaiming in our gum boots and rain slickers.

Roy was standing on the bank, his bike temporarily propped up on its kickstand. He seemed awestruck at the sheer force of nature, silent for once except to pick up sticks and pieces of wood, which he tossed into the wildly foaming waves. He watched with mouth agape as each chunk of debris slammed into the edge of the culvert and was pulled and sucked through the twisted metal rebar into its great black hole like hair going down the drain.

In the middle of this melee, Bart Wilson showed up and his general inclinations did not seem to be much diminished by the storm. We did not even hear him, until we turned around and saw him grinning at us like a Jolly Roger. He stepped forward and collared Ricky by the nape of the neck like a chicken. Jimmy and I instinctively huddled together, momentarily unsure of what to do. I moved forward as if to help and Jimmy held me fast by the arm. "Don't be an idiot," he spouted.

"Well, well—if it isn't my little fat friend. You know what day it is kid"? Bart mocked as we all drew back from what was unfolding in front of us. Ricky did not respond, he just looked back, bug-eyed. "It's *payday*, buttercup" Bart beamed with satisfaction. "You and your friends ready for a swim in the creek"?

I don't know if it was out of panic or opportunity, but Jimmy did something next which promised to either diffuse the action or add to it. Maybe it was an awkward attempt to cause a distraction. I turned my head and saw him inching toward Roy's bike, which was sitting there by the bank, propped up in the mud on its kick-stand. Jimmy took ahold of the bike, and as we stood there with our eyes fixed on Bart and Ricky he hoisted it toward the edge of the raging water. Roy and I both noticed at the same time, as Roy called out "My bike," and jumped to grasp it. I instinctively pushed Jimmy, trying to get him to drop the bike. In a moment all three of us, and the bike were swept into the frigid black deluge.

21

~

Flotsam and Jetsam

I slipped under the black rush of water, kicking and grasping in the shock of cold. The next moment, I slammed into the grate. My leg stabbed with pain. It was jammed up against the grate along with Roy's bike, pinned there by the force of the flow.

As I pulled myself free, I saw Roy beside me with his eyes wide open, gasping and holding onto his bike for dear life. Jimmy was floundering close by with water surging over his head, thrashing about with the abject panic which can possess those who are not strong swimmers. I instinctively reached out to grab him, and what happened next, took me by surprise. Instead of grasping my hand, he hit me squarely in the face with a blow which stunned me and sent me momentarily reeling under water. As I resurfaced tasting blood, I circled around Jimmy and took him with a choke hold from behind. We both struggled, our heads going under in unison, then bursting above the gushing waves as we fought each other and gasped for air. My leg throbbed with pain and at the same time I felt possessed of inhuman strength. I was holding Jimmy with an inchoate rage that might have hemorrhaged from the bowels of the earth on the day that Cain slew Abel. After a few minutes of intense struggle, Jimmy's head settled back limply in my grasp as time faded away into an inky cold blackness. I cannot remember in the end whether I was trying to kill Jimmy, or to save him. I only know that what happened lies in that no man's land somewhere between intention and unintended consequences.

I awoke in a hospital bed, with my leg elevated in a cast and my mother sitting beside me. When she saw me stir, she hasted to calm me down. "Mom, Roy? Jimmy?" I croaked. It seemed like my vocal cords were frozen and could not come alive. "Jacob," my mom hesitated, "don't worry. . . everything is going to be completely fine. They are both OK. Jimmy is alive" she hesitated, "he just has not woken up yet." I scanned the newspaper she had been reading by my bed. The headline read, "Local boys brush with death in near drowning." Roy it seems, had come through totally unscathed. The grand irony, is that grasping his bike had anchored him from being swept through the iron grate and drowned. There was also a picture of Jimmy from the yearbook with the explanation that he had suffered from lack of oxygen to the brain and was in a coma. It was yet unknown how bad the damage was, and whether he would recover his full faculties.

22

~

Swamp Water

An accident never seems to come out of just one thing. It is a random gathering of choices that on any given day might mean nothing. All those choices are like the drops of rain that seem inconsequential in isolation, but together they become a raging torrent. People seem to think that there is a safety in the grayness, which avoids the extremes of good and evil. They pull back toward the squishy middle, in an attempt to be safe by choosing to know only enough to get into trouble, but not enough to feel directly responsible. The grey zone was like our favorite drink, swamp water, which tried to get a taste of everything while choosing nothing in particular. And that is how accidents happen.

The only one really blessed with not knowing, was Roy. I could not decide whether this made him lucky or not. I realized that there is a weight that accompanies knowing, that makes you responsible even when you seem helpless. And that is how I felt when I thought back at all that had happened. It played over and over in my mind as I wondered what might have happened if I could have taken any part of it back.

Wishing was kind of like Ricky, having faith in all those ads. I thought about the story of Noah's ark, and wondered if God was really just holding his breath, waiting for mankind to finally decide what they liked better, good or evil. And all the while, people were holding their breath, waiting for some kind of ultimate justice from above. In that standoff where no one does anything, the rain starts and when it does you had better hope that neither you nor God blinks, because in that moment, the world can be swept away in a flood.

I turned my head to the pillow as both God and I cried.

23

~

Innocence

The next day my mother wheeled me over to see Jimmy who was on the same floor. I sat for a long time looking at what used to be my best friend, as the oxygen machine moved rhythmically up and down beside him. I looked at his face trying to ascertain what was going on inside, but he betrayed no aspect of an inner life whatsoever. He lay there unresponsive, blending in with the room as just another piece of intricate machinery draped in white.

I realized that even if Jimmy woke up he might not have any memory, and without that, he was incapable of friendship, or intention of any kind. For the first time, I realized, that Jimmy had an aspect to his appearance that I had never witnessed before. For the first time, he looked vaguely and completely innocent.

24

~

Transfiguration

The nurses kept telling me that I needed to get up and mobile. So, I took my crutch and started to hobble the various wards, shifting as much weight as I could bear on my cast. Maternity was bursting with visitors and pink and blue balloons, the sound of tiny babies crying in the background, and smelling vaguely like poop. The oncology ward smelled like strong medicine, and it seemed to be endless waiting rooms with stressed-looking people hooked up to IV's and others who seemed to be family members crammed into chairs. I made my way through to the coronary ward, which seemed quiet and serious. One name chalked on a board beside the door caught my attention. Winston Northey. I looked inside at the prostrate figure on the bed illuminated by the glow of the machinery and shrouded in white sheets. It was Moses, lying inert and hooked up to a bunch of wires.

I looked around. There did not seem to be any nurses, so I hobbled in and sat down by the bed. The heart monitor on the left gave testimony, while on the pallet Moses seemed to be like a dog in the middle of a turbulent dream, agitated and totally alert in an interior kind of way. He did not acknowledge my presence. I sat and watched his bushy eyebrows and his flowing white beard twitch. He seemed thin and somehow diminished. I studied him briefly, looking at his forearm, which was hooked up to the IV. There, what looked like a home-made tattoo was inscribed in thin capital letters without the benefit of illustration, *"prisoner of Jesus Christ."* I sat absorbed for a few minutes watching him as his chest rose and fell rhythmically, and then hobbled out the door to my own ward.

Back in the room, Moses trembled. As he lay on the bed, a dark brook from within his soul began to murmur. He seemed to be quoting from a lexicon burned deeply into memory.

> *"How long will ye vex my soul, and break me in pieces with words? These ten times have ye reproached me: are ye not ashamed that ye make yourselves strange to me? And be it indeed that I have erred, mine error remaineth with myself. If indeed ye will magnify yourselves against me and plead against me my reproach: Know now that God hath overthrown me, and hath compassed me with his net."*
> (JOB 19:2–6 KJV)

He paused, his face convulsed with inner passion. What appeared on the outside, the bulging veins on his forehead, and the animated movement beneath his eyelids, these were only ripples on the surface. The wattle on his neck quivered as the words continued to flow, only stronger.

> *"For I know that my redeemer liveth, and that he shall stand at the latter day upon the earth: And though after my skin worms destroy this body, yet in my flesh shall I see God: whom I shall see for myself, and mine eyes shall behold, and not another. . ."* (JOB 19:25–27 KJV)

He was quiet for a bit as if in deep petition. His hands flexed, and the great rigidity seemed to leave his body. He spoke again, and as he did, a single tear ran down his white cheek.

". . .. it doth not yet appear what we shall be: but we know that when he shall appear, we shall be like him; for we shall see him as he is." (1 JOHN 3:2 KJV)

It seemed that from a wilderness, Moses was finally approaching a promised land somewhere unknown to human imagination. A transfer was happening. Moses was arriving even as he departed. A beam of sunlight came through the window and his face was transfigured in the glow, bathed clean at last in a whiteness lighter than the air itself.

25

~

No Bite

My first day back at home, I had the strangest experience ever. I was out exercising my leg, limping past one of these big old houses with the wrap around porch when I heard a low growl. It was the gruff alert of a BIG dog in his most primordial state, when he senses an intruder. That intruder was me—limping along on my crutch, and, already sensing in grisly slow motion what was going to happen next. In the hundred yards between me and the dog, all I really saw was the glow of dog eyes, something I was already familiar with from my morning paper route. There was the head down, low gallop that only big dogs roll into. I heard the growl, visceral and menacing.

The house where the huge black dog was coming from was large and set back from the road. The dog had the further advantage of going downhill, and for a moment it seemed that he would get ahead of himself, his hind legs bounding faster than his front. I looked up on the porch, where a group of middle-aged men were drinking beer, and seeming totally unperturbed. One was pointing and the other was laughing. "Go get him, Lucifer," one guffawed.

Just like those dreams where you are being chased and you can only go in slow motion, the dog closed in on me and I could hear its snarling and growling as it attacked me from behind. I could feel its hot breath and cold slobber as its jaws closed over my calf and as I fell on the ground, I was vaguely aware of the owners literally doubled over in laughter up there on the deck. I could feel the dog chewing on my leg, like a carnivore over a fallen carcass, and yet there was no pain. I remembered how when you hurt yourself, the pain response sometimes arrives only much later. I looked down and suddenly realized what the dog owners were laughing about. That enormous black dog had no teeth. He was gumming my leg with everything he had, which was not much. This dog had no bite. He looked up at me as if betrayed.

Suddenly from the side, Roy sailed past us on his restored bike as if all was normal. "Look at my bike," he called out. "It's got everything. My Mom got it for me." He pedaled away happily to seek those with whom he could share his glad tidings as I collected myself and headed for home, limping, shaken and yet feeling somehow vindicated.

I was walking head down, thinking about what had happened when someone bumped into me roughly. I had forgotten all about Bart Wilson. After the accident I had half expected him to skulk off like a bad smell, but I was wrong. "Look out doofus" he jeered, driving the point of his shoulder into mine in a manner intended to inflict the most pain. I looked at him distastefully, not responding. "How's your friend the looney tunes?" he snorted. I paused and suddenly realized he was not talking about Roy, but Jimmy. It seemed that Bart was not at all sorry, in fact is seems he was disappointed only that he did not cause more harm. "Looney tunes," he mocked, "that kid's gone gooney. Hey, now he can hang out with the *other* half-wit," he laughed. Looking at Bart and the smirk on his face, I realized that no matter where I would go, there would always be a Bart somewhere. He was a dark potential that lurked in the shadows of life, perpetually waiting for an opportunity to inflict himself on the unsuspecting. But I was done with *this* Bart. As a bully, he should have known that the most significant transactions of life occur at the crossroads where choice and opportunity

meet. At this point I had a stiff wooden crutch in hand and nothing left to lose. Bart did not anticipate the handle of the crutch
as I drove it up under his nose. He staggered back, choking and
blubbering, cupping his face with both hands. He looked up from
his puerile display only in time to see the leg of the crutch swing
up with considerable force into his scrotum and in a moment, he
was doubled up on the side of the road like a deflated balloon,
choking and gasping for air, while cradling his family credentials
in both hands. As I walked away without looking back, it occurred
to me that the only reason Bart's petty reign of terror had been so
successful, was because none of us had ever thought to challenge
him. If good and evil could be treated like a zero-sum game, every
time we had ceded territory, he had become more powerful.

When I got home, Grandma told me about Moses. "Yes, I
was acquainted with Winston Northey when we were at school"
she said. "He was a fine picture of a man back then, him and his
sweetheart Mattie Walker, the class beauty. Now Mattie Walker
had the kind of beauty that needed to be redeemed on earth, but
Winston had his eyes set on redemption of a different sort. He had
plans for the ministry while she became a farm wife. All of that
came crashing down one day like a house of cards when he come
in from the field, and she was up and gone, run off with the hired
man. By the time he caught up with his bank account it was emptied out on the kind of high-toned living I guess she felt was her
due. People thought that was the end of it, but three months later,
Winston tracked them both down in a motel room, and he beat
that hired man like a rented mule, while Mattie sat on the bed, and
just screamed and screamed. He turned himself in to the police,
and she testified against him. Six months for assault. Sad thing was
that his prison record and broken marriage barred him from any
chance at the ministry. Winston Northey spent his life trying to
save others, but he could not even save himself."

Grandma paused to consider, then continued, "I estimate that
Winston should best have been a carpenter. His real gift was that
he liked to make things. Carpentry was about what he *loved*, not

what he opposed. You know, you can talk all day about what you are against, but when you *do* something, that's money in the bank. You know, you can put beautiful things into the world, if you've a mind to. There's not a lot of argument about it because you can see and touch what's been made. When a man makes something, he acts in the very image of God. That's a holy thing. Maybe holier than preaching, even."

26

~

The Course of a Stone

I was in the back yard, looking dolefully at Jimmy's house standing silently, as if announcing its desolation. Jimmy's near drowning had left him indefinitely impaired and his parents had shipped him to a care facility on the edge of town with breezy windows facing the sun, and a lot of quiet. Inside the kitchen, the light went on and I saw Jimmy's mom dressed up in a stylish black mini dress with a black mesh veil that riffed vaguely of Jacqueline Bouvier Kennedy in mourning. She picked up her matching black leather clutch, unclipped it for a moment, and pulled out a shiny compact flask, tilted her head and took a draught. Then she headed out the door, turned and looked at me without speaking, got into the car and backed out the driveway jerkily without looking behind her. She was going to the Country Club, where the requisite amount of attention from men in white golf pants and drinks with flags and sunny fruit slices, would insulate her black mood. Jimmy's mom was doing the best she could under the circumstances, being contemplative as only she knew how. Jimmy's dad had done what many people might do under tragic circumstances, the previous morning he had upgraded for a newer model that held no memory of the troubles that had plagued the old. He had giddily left town with the windows rolled down, leaving no forwarding address, and riding shotgun was the prim secretary whom he had recently hired, sporting a red head scarf and sunglasses. Jimmy's mom was beginning to discover feelings that she had rarely entertained simply because she never had to, and she wondered what she might buy next that would make her feel better.

When I turned around, Grandma was standing there in the yard behind me like a Daniel-come-to-judgement, with her arms crossed. She looked vexed. "Jacob, pick up that rock in front of you." She directed. "Grandma?" I said. "That rock in front of you on the edge of the garden there, pick it up," she repeated. I bent down and picked up the rock. "Now," said Grandma, "if you was to let go of that rock, do you have any reason to believe it would fall up instead of down"? "No," I said, confused. "Right," said Grandma, "I wanted to know that we weren't raising up a fool. A rock only falls one way and so does a man who chases after a well-turned ankle. I don't know those neighbors well, yet I have seen them a million times before. That man—his secretary is the latest shiny thing, in a line of shiny things. He says he wants a woman who understands him. What he *really* wants is a woman who *doesn't* understand him at all. If that girl at his office had any inkling who he really is, she'd run like hell the other way. You can't separate the character of a man from the things he does," she said. "To do so would be to defy the laws of gravity. It's a wise man who minds the course of a stone, for it only falls in one direction"!

Grandma snorted in disgust. She kicked the stone to the side of the garden, turned on her heel and headed back into the house.

27

~

Not Much Happens
in a Small Town

Not much happens in a small town. There are anonymous old men who come down to the train station to see the trains come and go. They silently watch the passengers disembark as if they are waiting for someone, and then leave again without adequate explanation, only to return again the next day. The world turns very slowly when it is bounded by tidy green lawns on every horizon, and people join bridge clubs and bowling leagues as a way of temporary escape. Boredom lies thick upon a new day, like dew that refuses to rise up and be dispersed. Once the prosaic business of the day is done, when the crickets start to chirp, and the streetlights come on, teenagers build bonfires and have impromptu tailgate parties in farmers' fields. On Friday nights, armed with a .22 and a case of beer, they will trail out to the furthest borders of nowhere, to shoot out the glass insulators of the hydro wires which line the long country roads. If you asked them why they do this, they would stare at you blankly as if not understanding the question. If the Devil indeed makes work for idle hands, then a small town after five o'clock should be his very own factory.

As if nature was on cue, somewhere in the gathering dusk a coyote, mangy-looking and skinny, circled a young fawn that was bleating, looking about in a panic for its mother. Its hind leg was caught in a bear trap. The coyote had no concept of mercy—it knew only the gnawing in its own belly and it sensed what a predator looks for, weakness and opportunity. The bleating panic of the fawn intensified as the coyote closed in, circling, checking the wind—its natural cautiousness encouraged by the good fortune that no natural competition had stumbled across the fawn sooner. When the farmer arrived, he could not forget the look in the fawn's eyes. Despite his dispassionate years as a hunter, and butcherer of cattle there was something about the coyote's slow-motion singularity of purpose which twisted in the farmer's gut. When he had butchered pigs, the blow of the mallet had been swift and merciful. As if in contrast, the coyote had positioned itself comfortably to a leisurely dinner, no matter that its prey was alive and witness to its own slow-motion demise. The coyote's nose was covered in blood as it dived into the softest parts of the fawn's living entrails, pulling out pieces of slippery organ and palpitating tissue, licking the blood and jerkily gulping down the glistening morsels. The fawn's eyes twitched at every tear in its flesh, too feeble to provide an adequate response. The farmer's shotgun roared, and the coyote yelped for a moment, then fell prostrate. The second charge of the shotgun mercifully ended the plight of the fawn as the farmer placed the barrel in between its eyes, still shimmering with life, and pulled the trigger.

Later on that night when he put his toddlers to bed, he told the same stories he had heard as a child, of gingerbread, and innocence, and the shared apprehension that somewhere out there, predators must be adequately met by those who wish to survive. As he read again the part where the hunter kills the wolf, he tried to erase what he had seen that day from his brain. His children laughed and clapped and wanted to hear the story again. They did not fully comprehend what he was talking about. A part of him celebrated their innocence and an equal part felt an urgency that they should know what he already knew.

On the far side of town, someone in a hooded jacket peered surreptitiously through the side window of the gas station. The somewhat portly cashier who appeared to be about sixteen, was reading a gossip magazine at the counter and eating a bag of chips into which her chubby fingers dived with apparent muscle memory. On the floor before the door, was a black lab who looked more to be sleeping than standing guard. The hooded figure took a screwdriver from his back pocket and quietly jimmied the lock on the back of the store. After a few tries, the latch clicked and gave way, the door swung partially open, and the hooded figure slipped in like a shadow. He passed through the stock room and peered out through the crack in the door, watching the girl absorbed in her reading. He quietly took a pack of beef jerky from a stock bin, and ripped it open with his teeth. Inside the store, the dog took notice, lifting its nose to a foreign scent, and testing the wind for what would come next.

28

~

Predator

The girl suddenly started at the same moment that the dog gave a low growl. "Easy, doggy," said the intruder. "You want jerky"? He extended the open bag and tossed one piece onto the floor. The dog greedily snapped up the morsel, and looked up, waiting for more. "Here boy," the intruder said, encouraging. He advanced on the dog, gauging its response as he crept forward. The girl who had been standing with her mouth agape, suddenly found her voice. "I know you," she said woodenly in an accusing voice. "Your name is Bart. I've heard about you. You're in my sister's home room. What do you want, anyway"? Bart by this time had circled close to the dog, whose nose was now buried in the bag of beef jerky. He pulled a sack from the inside of his jacket, and quickly threw it over the dog's head. The dog yelped. Bart pulled the drawstring tight and clamped the struggling animal under his armpit while grappling with its thrashing limbs. The girl screamed, but it was too late.

Not much goes on in a small town. Not much at all. So, a police car with cherry top blazing is news. So is a fire engine fast in pursuit. Small children poured out onto the street from the family dinner table, oblivious to the protests of their mothers, doors opened a crack, and window shades lifted as people noted the emergency vehicles speeding by. The police radio crackled. "Ten-thirty-one alert. Ninth Line and Bailey side road. Do you copy"? The portly police officer pressed the button. "Officer Barley. I copy. On it." He pressed the pedal of the cruiser harder as he hit the edge of town by the highway. Behind him the fire engine blared its horn, and all of nature jumped at the unexpected intrusion to the quiet. Far in the distance, a red glow could be seen rising up from the horizon.

Officer Barley was a seasoned policeman and he thought he had seen everything. But some days, are not like any other and this was one of them. When he arrived at the scene of the fire, all he could hear was the anguished baying of a hound. He ducked through the front door, then a moment later erupted from the entrance with an awkward cargo writhing in his grasp. The shapeless bundle thrashed and fell, slippery with blood, onto the pavement. The officer bent over in the parking lot and vomited. It was not from smoke inhalation.

29

~

Intent

There is something about crime which fascinates the general public. When something spectacular happens, newspapers sell out, and people in barber shops gather and gossip about the details. So it was with this particular court case. Bart Wilson was in custody, charged with arson and attempted murder. The fat girl in the gas station had been tied up when he started the fire. It was not that she was physically damaged, it was what she sobbed to her mother once she had been taken home from the police station. After emptying out the cash register and filling his pockets with cigarettes, Bart had carelessly tossed a match on the magazine rack by the door. As the flames rose up he turned to the girl and laughed. "Barbecue time, porky," was all he said before running out into the darkness of the night. But that was not the part which garnished the most discussion. It was what the officer had reported about the skinned dog. "Why would he hang around to skin a dog after he killed it?" asked one man in the barber shop. "Well, that's the point," said his barber. "The dog was not dead when he skinned it. He tied the girl up and made her watch. Now that's something you sure as Hell can't un-see! When they caught up with that kid, he had broken into a cottage. There were dishes and empty beer bottles strewn all over the floor. He was sitting on the couch watching TV and eating a baloney sandwich like nothing had happened. The police officers had never seen anything like it"!

The inevitable question that comes up next is "Why"? People offer unedited conjecture. "My wife taught him in grade one," said Tom Greene. "Couldn't get a single straight word out of the kid. Said he just lied all the time." "That a fact?" answered Bill Irving. "My Mom was a school teacher too, and she had this thing. She always said lying leads to murder. People would laugh, but it was like this. Lying goes to cheating, cheating goes to stealing, stealing goes to violence, and violence goes to murder. I never forgot it. It all starts with a tiny lie." "It must be because of his upbringing," said Mabel Brown. "The poor boy needs some good mothering, bless his heart!" she had declared. "I think he is just misunderstood." Her husband Hank cut her off. "Mabel, I think you are wrong," he offered. "I think I understand that kid very well. I was the same way at that age. What that boy needs, is a good fathering like the kind my dad gave me out back of the woodshed. That's what put me off a life of crime. My dad wore out my bad intentions the old-fashioned way. When I dropped out of school he put me to work with him, where he could keep an eyeball on me."

Bart himself had offered a more succinct reply across the desk when the same question was posed to him by a county-appointed social worker. "Why did I do it?" he asked facetiously. "Why not? Nobody stopped me, did they? Weak people suck. They should just die. 'Whah, Whah, oh *Bart*, why are you doing this to me? Why don't you just let me go,' he mocked? That fat bitch is just pathetic. Should have just let me torch her. So, when do I get out of here? I want a Coke. I want a cigarette. Hey! Are they going to put my picture in the paper"? The social worker scratched on her pad and wondered how she would word her assessment in official jargon for something which might look like a viable rehabilitation plan. After all, everyone wants to be redeemed, right?

Ricky, Kevin and I gathered at the treehouse, buzzing over a crumpled newspaper and reading over what had happened. "Man, that guy is one mean mother," said Kevin as if in admiration. "I didn't know he had it in him." Ricky was not so sanguine. He looked sick as he pulled out a letter. We thought it might be some other kind of failed offer he had sent for in the mail. The letter was postmarked from the county prison, and inside the envelope, was a piece of paper with a few words scrawled across the page with a thick black marker. "Don't think you got off" said the note. "When I get out of here you and your friends your all ded meet." "Guys," said Ricky, quivering. "we're screwed. They're going to turn that psycho loose as soon as he makes bail. Maybe we should run away and leave town." "Wow," said Kevin in an affected tone. "That kid for sure cannot spell." Ricky looked at us, pale and wan, wondering in the back of his mind whether his lucky rabbit's foot he had sent away for would afford him any protection. Like an unlucky penny, Bart would turn up again. You could count on it.

30

~

Whack-a-Mole

B art Wilson was a strong believer in justice. The problem was that his was of the playground variety, a childish account which kept track of personal slights, whether real or imagined. What mattered to Bart was respect. Accordingly, to settle accounts meant only one thing—revenge, the kind which would strike fear into those who challenged him. When he got out, he had some business to attend to. First on his list were those smart-ass kids. He had already dealt with Jimmy. But that fat little pisser Ricky, his friend Kevin, and especially Jacob, the skinny kid who had squared him with the crutch—they were all in line for some serious payback.

Inside the detention center, Bart Wilson did what Bart Wilson usually did. He raised hell. His mettle was tested just like any other inmate when he landed in the general population. If it is true that there is no valor among thieves, it might also be true that there is no real camaraderie, just a sizing up for where you stand in the pecking order. When he came into the cafeteria for his first lunch session, he scanned up and down the aisles warily, walking with his tray, trying to figure out where he could sit. An inmate at a crowded table gestured theatrically, beckoning him over. When

Bart approached, the man stood up and grandstanded. "Well, it's the local celeb" he said, "shouldn't you be eating barbecue"? The other inmates who were watching, hooted. "Maybe some barbecued chicken. You like chicken kid? I like chicken. I like it a *lot*. Some people call me a chicken hawk. In fact, I think I am going to be having some chicken tonight." He laughed and most of the men around the table laughed too. Bart stood at the edge of the table. He did not look flummoxed. Instead, he abruptly hurled his hot meal into the face of his provocateur. The man howled, shocked and tried to claw the steaming food out of his eyeballs. Now a tray may seem like a clumsy weapon. When it is swung flat, it cannot do much damage. But sideways, it can be a thing of force. Bart sliced his food tray in a clean arc through the air across the table. Its corner hit the self-professed chicken hawk flat in the teeth. Blood and incisors sprayed everywhere. The table company parted like the Red Sea, and Bart leaped over the divide and in a moment, he was upon the man. Instead of facing him, he wrapped both legs around the man's waist from behind like a monkey riding a donkey. The man stumbled back and grappled in the air, trying to get a hold on his assailant, while Bart pummeled from behind with both fists in a hail of blows that fell faster than a whack-a-mole game. There was a popping sound when one of his blows broke the man's nose. It gushed with blood. The man had not been able to land even a single punch in return. Overcome, he soon slumped to the ground and Bart spat on him and administered one last coup de grace with a boot to the head. When he looked up, the watching inmates parted slightly, pulling back as if by reflex. Bart smiled. He ended up that evening in solitary confinement for the sake of general order. The jail staff did not know that a chance to be alone was exactly what Bart was aiming for. He had heard that it was going to rain. "A rain storm" he thought to himself, "Just like in all the movies. It's a perfect time for a jail break."

31

~

Stormy Monday

Inside the jail, someone's transistor radio trailed off into the night with music interspersed with periodic crackles of static. The radio host's voice rose up cheerily. ". . . that was T-Bone walker with a real blues classic—Stormy Monday. And that's what it is my friends, a stormy Monday! In case you didn't check the weather folks, it's time to get out the umbrellas and stay out of those open fields"! In terms of a storm, this was a full-fledged electrical one that were it a black and white movie, could have raised up Frankenstein. The wind outside howled like a lost soul. Bart sat in his cell with satisfaction, listening to the rain beat on the wall, and watching the flashes of white as they lit up the dark interior. The cell window had chipped paint flaked all around it, a visual commentary on the state of the underlying concrete and the effervescence that was eating away at it. He stuck the metal shaving mirror to the handle of the mop with a piece of gum and held it up to the window so that he could get a view outside. There was a metal drainpipe and it ran all the way down the prison wall to the grass below. "Suckers" thought Bart to himself. He started to count the timing between the flashes of lightning and the ensuing thunder. He then pulled out the metal mattress frame from the cot and hoisted it above his head like a battering ram. From the far side of the room, he watched for the lightning flash, counted to ten, then charged forward and crashed the bed against the metal grate at the same moment the thunder pealed. He waited for the next flash and repeated his assault on the window. Eventually, the metal started to nudge forward, loosening itself from the punky concrete which surrounded it. A bolt pulled loose. Flakes of softened cement fell down to the floor below. After a few more crashes of thunder, the window bars gave way and plummeted to the ground outside the cell leaving a gaping wound in the edifice. Bart took his hand towel from the sink and doubled it around his neck. He leaned the bed frame against the wall on an angle, bracing it on both sides with bed sheets tied to the cell fixtures, then cautiously started to climb his improvised ladder, leaning against the wall to stabilize himself. His fingertips were just short of the opening. Bart gave a cautious leap and managed to gain an edge. His hands grasped the opening and he pulled himself upward. Perched inside the window like a cat burglar, he scanned the courtyard. There was a drop of about thirty feet to the grass below. Too much to risk breaking a leg, but if he was careful, he could make his way down the drainpipe which was two feet over by the end of the ledge. Bart edged over and gingerly took the hand towel from around his neck and twisted it into as narrow a bundle as he could, aided by the wetness of the rain. On the third swing, he managed to pass one edge of the twisted towel under the drainpipe. It was now or never. Bart swung out from the ledge, simultaneously reaching for the other end of the towel as he started to drop. There was a jolt as his full weight jerked against the drainpipe and he slipped downward for a moment. The pipe creaked and strained on its bolts while Bart held his breath and braced his legs against the wall, pressing his feet into the crevices in the brickwork to stabilize himself. He doubled the towel ends around his wrists for extra support and paused to gather strength for the descent.

Bart could be a clever teen. He was inventive and could improvise when the situation called for it. But he had sadly failed science class. That part about electricity, conductivity, and lightning seeking metal and high spots in the landscape like trees and flagpoles, to discharge its excess, that was for egg-heads and losers to sweat about. The white-hot bolt struck him with the force of a truck. His teeth clamped together and snapped like chalk at the same moment that his hair stood out straight from his scalp and erupted in a plume of fire. His hands involuntarily gripped the wet towel as one million volts of white hot light ran from the metal pipe and coursed through his body. Bart's short career of crime faded as he plummeted to the ground below, and a putrid smell akin to Sulphur floated through the air. Except that the force of the lightning strike had burst his eardrums, somewhere in the blackness of night, he might have overheard a malevolent voice laughing.

32

≈

Now What?

It was a good week for news. The daily paper sold out fast, and people gathered together scanning pictures of Bart's body covered with a cloth, behind the line of yellow tape. Some girls at school cried. One claimed that Bart had been her boyfriend. She became an instant celebrity and the news channel even interviewed her. "He was so brave," she said. "I'm the only one who really understood him." She wiped a tear from her eye and checked her makeup mirror to see how she looked as the cameras rolled. Her mother stood by in the background, looking protective and proud. "I'm her mother," she smiled and nodded looking around, to the attention of no one in particular.

The papers also scoured the school for any teacher who would give commentary. "What would you say about his temporary life of crime?" one reporter demanded. "Would you say that high schools are failing to prepare students for real life"? The teacher looked at the reporter, cocked her hand on her hip and answered back. She seemed to be angry. "Honey, I teach at a high school. Four short years that are supposed to stand in for eighteen years of parenting. They are waiting to get out into real life you think? You know what? *All* of life is real life. Even high school. There isn't any other kind. You know what you saw today? Real life's cure for stupid, that's what. Temporary? You know what I can tell you about temporary? *Life* is temporary. Bart is just the latest poster boy for that. You could say, he had all the same chances as anybody else, but he made all the wrong choices. Consider that the lesson for the day," she noted before turning on her heel and walking away.

As things go in a small town, my mom happened to be distantly acquainted with Bart's mother and felt she must be seen paying her respects in case she bumped into her in the future. When I arrived home, she informed me that I must go with her to the funeral parlor where the family was having a visitation. That was the last place I wanted to be. "Better bring a bathing suit and some sun tan lotion when you go," my Gran called out. "You know if you are going where that kid is, it's going to be plenty hot"!

When we arrived, a long gauntlet of people was already lined up waiting to offer condolences—although in truth, many were there simply to gawk. Bart's parents were at the front shaking hands, and in the back of the room behind them was Bart's school portrait, propped up on a stand beside a pine casket and a display of flowers. In the picture he wore a sardonic smile that now seemed somewhat creepy, and he looked almost respectable in a newly-pressed denim shirt dressed up with a bolero tie. I shuffled up to the line, wanting to funnel through as quickly as possible. My stomach churned, and I tried not to look at the casket. "Thank you, thank you. My boy, he was my best friend." Bart's mother wiped her eyes, talking to a woman in the lineup. "I worked my fingers to the bone to give him everything he ever wanted, and Lord knows I would have given more if I could." "That's right, it was never enough," Bart's dad mumbled from the side. "We spoiled that kid and now look what happened." "*Vern*," hissed his wife. "You can't talk about my boy that way." She was talking over him as if nobody else was there. "If you had pushed for a promotion like I said, you could have provided like a *real* man. I told him never to be like you. He wouldn't take orders from *anybody*. He was going to *be* somebody, someday." She started to cry.

Bart's dad stood there looking dull and defeated. I had just expected that given Bart's nature, the apple didn't fall far from the tree. I imagined that his dad would be a sailor or a lumber jack or something tough, but it seems like he had soft hands and he was skinny and mild-looking. "Gert, all that overtime," he said plaintively. "It's like our lives got burned up in a puff of smoke with that kid. We didn't do him right though. There was plenty of things that kid needed to hear but you wouldn't have it. Even when he was out raising hell, he could do no wrong. That's how we wound up *here*." Bart's mom snorted in anger. She turned and stormed out of the room like a black whirlwind, leaving her husband standing there awkwardly looking back and forth at the whispering guests. Pastor Winters stepped in to catch the fumble. "Bless you, he'll be missed," he said, shaking hands. "He was a good boy, thank you, yes." The minister stood glad-handing the people who were next in line. I fled the room and stood in the cool dark outside. There were tears streaming down my face because I was so angry. I was incensed at the utter waste, that life could be used up with such thoughtless contempt that a preacher had to offer up platitudes and lies to make it better.

The next day in my tree fort, Kevin, Ricky and I poured through the newspaper, which was filled front to back with every angle of the Bart story. "Hey Ricky, I guess you're off the hook" I noted. "I guess we all are. Now what are you guys going to do"? I suddenly realized that all of the things that had happened had awakened something inside of me, a growing hunger to live, and that my life should account for something. We were just a bunch of kids, sitting around playing with dumb stuff and wasting away our time. Ricky looked at me and scratched his head like he didn't understand the question. "*You* know Jacob," he said. "Like I *always* do. Maybe I'll order something. Something *new* that you guys never saw before. Maybe I'll get the Sea Monkeys this time. "Do?" asked Kevin in response to the same question. "Why should I do anything?" he scoffed, "like, who's going to make me? I'm just going to hang out. Babes and beers and fighting the man. That's *my* future."

I don't know why, but at the end of that day, I walked all the way out to the graveyard on the edge of town and I sat on the foot of my father's grave for a long time, tracing my finger over his middle name which was the same as my own. I thought about Bart's shadow of a dad. Having a dad at home who wouldn't man up might be almost as bad a deal as having a good dad who was dead. No matter what I could still remember all the good stuff my dad did and maybe even imitate him. Some things needed to be decided. I think I walked away from the grave that day, as the beginnings of a man.

33

~

Wakeup Call

I dreamed of my father. He was leaning over his tool chest, pack-ing the tools away as if finishing up a job, surrounded in a halo of ethereal white. "Dad?" I said cautiously. "Is it you"? When I approached to embrace him, he stood, turned and looked at me without speaking, then suddenly pushed me back roughly. I gath-ered myself, shaken and approached him again. "Dad?" I said, cau-tiously. "What are you doing? Are you playing"? I was starting to panic, and I could hear my heart racing. I didn't know what was going on. He raised both fists up in a ready fighting stance. "Come at me" he said. I ran at him with all my strength and in return received a box in the head which sent me reeling back. "Fight" he said, "You have it in you." "Dad, what are you doing?" I asked, hurt and aggrieved. "Come at me" he insisted, "Show me what you've got." "Dad I can't," I cried, "you're too strong for me." "Yes, you can," he said. "You *have* to." This time I ran in and hit him as hard as I could, pounding away with both fists. He pinned my arms so that his face was a foot away from my own and we grappled like two gladiators in close quarters. We were eyeball to eyeball, each trying to expiate our various positions and gain the advantage. There is a moment in every epic struggle which winds down to the realization that you are going to have to eventually release your adversary and take your chances. Only I did not want to let go. It felt too much like goodbye. My father dissolved from my grasp, leaving me alone. There are parts of life which leave behind an empty space for words unspoken. Your only recourse for emancipation, is to live out those words alone as best you know how.

I sat up in bed wounded and shaken, thinking of all the various kinds of evil in the world—the capricious and random force of nature daring anyone to get in its way; the careless like Jimmy, and the hungry like Oscar the fish. But the evil that troubled me the most was that which made the least sense because it was unnecessary, and impossible without human complicity. It came as a dark and foreign implant on nature that could grow only if ignored, like a weed hidden in a garden.

I figured that people are messed up in ways they can't admit, not even to themselves. And that is where malice comes from—the kind of sin that is not just a mistake or an accident but is willingly blind. It happens when people double down on their own worst tendencies instead of accepting blame. They end up like Bart Wilson, bashing on other people just for fun because it's easier than trying to fix themselves.

I thought about Jesus dying on the cross. If God had a big plan, then why did the Devil still give it his best shot, even though he knew he would be defeated in the end? I guessed the Devil was so jealous that it didn't much matter to him how things turned out as long as he could just wreak some havoc along the way. The Devil also has bastard children among the sons of men. They roam this earth refusing to believe they are guilty, and they are the ones of whom the world should perhaps be most afraid.

I finally understood something of my father, that men are made for goodness, but they have to choose it. They have to look the snake in the eye and hand back that shiny apple. My father chose to get used up for something good, despite all the things that were stacked up against him. All those people out there standing on the sidelines waiting for a better ride, they missed what my father already knew—that the best way to live, might start with learning how to die.

A moment in time flickered through my brain, when I once asked my Dad, "What's the best thing you ever did"? He ruffled my hair and said, "You are." In that moment I had a brief vision of eternity and how it is that things don't really end, they are just passed on. They are hopes and dreams put into trust.

34

~

The Limp

"And Jacob was left alone; and there wrestled a man with him until the breaking of the day. And when he saw that he prevailed not against him, he touched the hollow of his thigh; and the hollow of Jacob's thigh was out of joint, as he wrestled with him. And he said, let me go, for the day breaketh. And he said, I will not let thee go, except thou bless me. And he said unto him, What is thy name? And he said, Jacob. And he said, Thy name shall be called no more Jacob, but Israel: for as a prince hast thou power with God and with men, and hast prevailed. And Jacob asked him, and said, Tell me, I pray thee, thy name. And he said, Wherefore is it that thou dost ask after my name? And he blessed him there. And Jacob called the name of the place Peniel: for I have seen God face to face, and my life is preserved. And as he passed over Penuel the sun rose upon him, and he halted upon his thigh."

–GENESIS 32:24–31 (KJV)

There is a new seed for hope. It sleeps in the memory of the dead whose burden we carry. We who live on share their secrets, and the truth is that I am guilty. Opening my eyes in the world and breathing its air has made me culpable.

Being guilty as I see it, might be my best defense. In fact, it may be the only hope left, because every person who tastes Eden's apple, will come to know the difference between good and evil. Truly, the innocent have no reason to care. They have no skin in the game. It will fall on the guilty and the bruised to bear us forward. For those who have died and for those yet to be born, we bear this care into the world, though in pain as one in childbirth.

Life, it seems to turn both backwards and forwards at once, like the crazy wheels on Roy's bike. It drives on into the future while gazing backwards in consultation of memory. The only chance it has to stand still, are those erratic moments of choice and in those brief points of arbitration, life is weighed, verdicts are considered, and the flood waters stand watching just for a moment. It seems that both God and Mankind are considering their options and hoping that no one blinks. Our choices, they weigh into the future as either millstones, or anchors for those who will follow.

I arise from my bed, get dressed and prepare to deliver my morning newspapers. The sky outside is showing signs of rain. I do not bundle up. Instead I walk out into it gratuitously, though limping. In the deluge that follows, the path of my footsteps is washed as a muddy tributary that flows into the great river. I see the promise of a distant rainbow on the horizon and as I walk without fear into the fury of the storm, I am baptized anew, thinking about the man that I should become.

35

~

Confession

The space of a generation and more has passed since the events of that summer. I have been a minister of the Lord for over thirty years now, and I have seen seasons of repentance come and go. I have blessed crying babies, tied couples together in bonds of love, and talked more than a few people from the ledge of life. I have also wept great drops of blood in the night that no one has seen, for God Himself has wounded me and that wound has been my salvation. The wound is the knowledge of the truth which abides behind the shiny exterior people show at Church, that what separates us, and a murderer might be a mere moment of decision or a single lie.

I should know. That summer, it seemed like the enemy was without, that we were all battling Bart Wilson. Who was right and wrong was a black and white affair. But on the secret underbelly of it all, part of me could not stand Jimmy and wished him ill. Now I wonder in the middle of the night about the damage I might have caused, and I guess I will never be sure until God Himself reveals the day. People sometimes slap me on the back and tell me that I am a good guy. What seems more likely is that I am simply trying to make amends.

Sometimes people ask me if I think I will ever lose my faith. What I have seen has braced me with the kind of truths you need to fight a battle, one that I see change shape, vanish and materialize yet again like a grinning chameleon. People like to be fooled, to think they are good but I know that to save humanity took an act of God, and it will take an act of God yet, to see it to the end.

I have been accused of entering the ministry in search of a missing father. It is true that I had to go looking for my father after he died. But God found me all on His own. He needed one who understood what was at stake, and what it would cost us all if even one man failed to see with his eyes wide open and stand in the gap. People who imagine that the world has no more use for men, have not been paying attention. There are words which women like to hear, the kind that flatter and with which a serpent set the world on end. But men should be made of sterner stuff. I am grateful that I had a good father. A good father will not try to save you, because he cannot; but he will gird your loins about with truth in preparation for the road ahead.

During the years of my ministry, I have had the opportunity to check in on Jimmy. Both of us are sporting a thatch of grey hair and we age with a shared secret whose verdict will be revealed only in its appointed time. In these forty years, Jimmy has not spoken, although he smiles a lot.

During my last visit, Jimmy finally broke his silence, if only for an instant. I was sitting by his bed looking at him when suddenly he sat up in a moment of lucidity, turned and pointed his finger at me with a jester's grin. He only uttered five words and they bore the weight of a gavel. "I know who you are" he proclaimed. Then he turned back and looked out the window.

The wisdom of fools, can be frightening.

"For the preaching of the cross is to them that perish foolishness; but unto us which are saved it is the power of God. For it is written, I will destroy the wisdom of the wise, and will bring to nothing the understanding of the prudent. Where is the wise? where is the scribe? where is the disputer of this world? hath not God made foolish the wisdom of this world? For after that in the wisdom of God the world by wisdom knew not God, it pleased God by the foolishness of preaching to save them that believe. For the Jews require a sign, and the Greeks seek after wisdom: But we preach Christ crucified, unto the Jews a stumbling block, and unto the Greeks foolishness; But unto them which are called, both Jews and Greeks, Christ the power of God, and the wisdom of God. Because the foolishness of God is wiser than men; and the weakness of God is stronger than men."

–FIRST CORINTHIANS 1:18–25

Epilogue

~

The Sower of Tares

"The kingdom of heaven is likened unto a man which sowed good seed in his field: But while men slept, his enemy came and sowed tares among the wheat, and went his way. But when the blade was sprung up, and brought forth fruit, then appeared the tares also. So the servants of the householder came and said unto him, Sir, didst not thou sow good seed in thy field? from whence then hath it tares? He said unto them, an enemy hath done this."

—MATTHEW 13: 24–28 (KJV)

It was just another dreary day, plodding from sun to sun, with the usual characters carrying out their usual routines. A business man, dressed in a nondescript grey suit, was driving home, steeped in reverie. Going to and from work was the part of his day least likely to be spoiled because it was an hour of spinning dreams that had not yet been tested by reality. When the man was at work, he yearned to be idle, and yet when free at home he was burdened with a nagging sense of things left undone. The only rest from such scrutiny was that lazy hour-long commute, fueled with the credit of good intentions and yet free from the judgements that must accompany arrival. Lost in this endless oscillation between points, he did not see the sports car rearing up behind him. It passed him on the dirt road, spraying gravel in its wake and forcing him to swerve into the shoulder. After a loud crash, a cloud of dust and smoke enveloped the man, who awoke from his torpor in stunned disbelief. He was not dead, technically at least. In fact, he felt more alive than he had felt in a long time. It was ironic that the first thing of consequence that he had run into in years, was the tree trunk staring at him through the broken windshield. That was because the tree trunk just happened to be real.

The sports car was driven by Jimmy's dad, who laughed when he saw the car go off the road. "Loser!" he crowed, looking back in his rear-view mirror. His secretary giggled beside him. "Baby I like your style," she purred, "I just love a man who goes out and takes what he wants."

Meanwhile in town, a balding and pudgy geriatric straddled a riding lawn mower, with a cigar clenched in his teeth like General MacArthur and armed with an odd mechanical apparatus strapped to his back. It was a cobbled-together equivalent of a flamethrower, derived from a large propane canister equipped with a hose and a long welding gun that emitted a jet of fire from its mouth when depressed. Since returning home from the war, his post-traumatic stress played out in a daily vendetta against the encroaching weeds. He would patrol the lawn, spouting bursts of flame whenever he saw a golden head poking forth. "Die, you goddamned krauts, die. . ." he muttered to himself through gritted teeth. "Why do they keep coming back, dammit"?

In another borough not far away, more colorful news seemed destined in the form of a hippie love-in, planned on a leafy vacant lot by the edge of town. The hippies' intention was to get naked to protest the war in Vietnam. It seemed like a sexy idea because it involved no real work and denouncing something gave them the thrill of a real moral stance. They were not really for anything either, but that was a detail which did not seem to matter much to the excited participants. Together they formed a formidable bicycle convoy, free of attire but clothed in virtue. Their naked entourage flopped and jiggled awkwardly past the home of Roy, who stood mesmerized in his front yard, when he saw the long line of bicycles approach. "Mom, it's a bicycle parade," he called out, as he stripped down to nothing but his thick glasses and joined the queue. "I'm going to be king of the bicycles"! he chortled in glee. Honking his horn from the rear, he followed in naked bliss to wherever it was they might be going.

The vacant lot on the edge of town seemed to smile in anticipation of its impending guests. After the recent conflagration of Kevin and crew, nature was recovering slowly but surely as leaves and vines crept into place so inauspiciously as to go almost unnoticed. As the first naked cyclist approached, a small green sprout simultaneously pushed its way toward the light, bursting forth from the earth with a determined will of its own. At this stage it looked just like any other youthful sprig poking its head out into the world. If it was a good plant, or an interloper, no one could yet tell. The haunting question remained, whether a man could be found left in the world who would be worthy to judge.

> "Every man's work shall be made manifest: for the day shall declare it, because it shall be revealed by fire; and the fire shall try every man's work of what sort it is."
>
> –FIRST CORINTHIANS 3:13 (KJV)

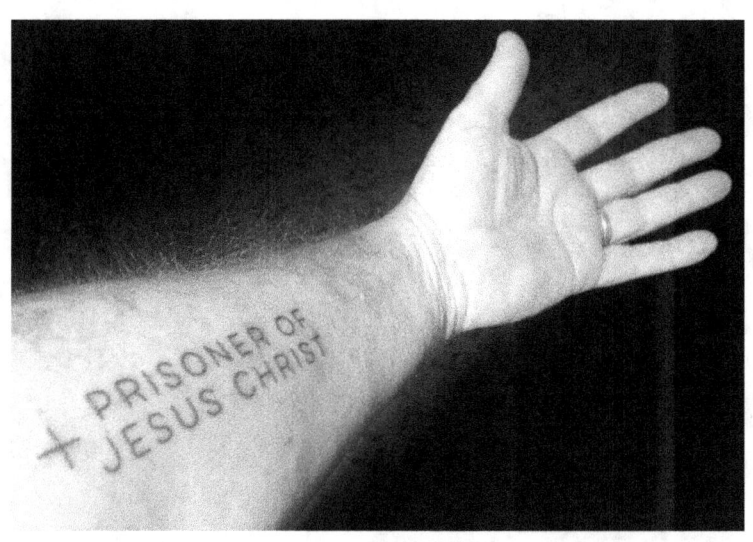

www.ingramcontent.com/pod-product-compliance
Lightning Source LLC
Chambersburg PA
CBHW070827250626
47170CB00006B/2238